THE DREAM TRAVELER'S
Game
THE WARRIOR AND THE ARCHER

THE DREAM TRAVELER'S SERIES
——— BOOK 6 ———

TED DEKKER & H.R. HUTZEL

ISBN 979-8-9865173-9-1 (Paperback Edition)

Also available in the Dream Travelers Game series

The Boy and his Song (Book 5)
ISBN 979-8-9865173-8-4 (Paperback Edition)

Out of the Darkness (Book 7)
ISBN 979-8-9888509-0-8 (Paperback Edition)

Also available in the Dream Travelers Quest series (the prequel)

Into the Book of Light (Book 1)
ISBN 978-0-9968124-6-7 (Paperback Edition)

The Curse of Shadow Man (Book 2)
ISBN 978-0-9968124-7-4 (Paperback Edition)

The Garden and the Serpent (Book 3)
ISBN 978-0-9968124-8-1 (Paperback Edition)

The Final Judgement (Book 4)
ISBN 978-0-9968124-9-8 (Paperback Edition)

Published by:
Scripturo
PO Box 2618
Keller, Texas 76248

Cover art and design by Manuel Preitano

Printed in the United States of America

Chapter One

ANNELEE STOOD AND BRUSHED her hands on her thighs. Tucking a strand of hair behind her ears, she narrowed her gaze and stared at Theo. "Is it really you?" Her face lit up with recognition before he could respond. "Oh my gosh, it is you!" She ran to him, closing the distance between them in seconds, then wrapped her arms around him and squeezed. A familiar smell overtook him—strawberry lip balm. He hugged her back. Memories overwhelmed him as he breathed in her scent.

She held him for a long moment before pulling back. When she did, Theo realized he now stood a whole head taller than her.

"I can't believe it. I haven't seen you in a year and a half, and now here you are." Her hands lingered on his arms. "And look how tall you are! Gosh, you look so different. Like a ..." She hesitated. "Like a man."

Heat flushed Theo's cheeks. He hadn't seen Annelee since he hit his growth spurt.

"Aren't you going to say something?" she asked.

Theo cleared his throat. "Oh, uh, you've grown too. I mean, you've changed—in a good way." He scratched his head, then clarified. "You look great."

A smile flickered on her lips, then faded. "I was so sad to hear the news about your dad."

The empathy in her eyes unraveled him. He pulled in a slow, measured breath to compose himself.

As if sensing he needed a moment, Annelee dropped her hands from his arms and wandered toward the center of the Waystation.

Theo's mind raced. His tongue fumbled for words, but before he could get anything out, Annelee turned and asked, "So how did you end up here?"

He swallowed.

She looked even prettier than he remembered.

"Talya."

She nodded. "Me too. I was playing on my sister's PlayStation when a Roush pulled me through the screen."

"Same," Theo said. Questions swarmed his mind. "So, in reality, where are we? I mean, we're here in our minds, but I must still be in my room at my grandmother's house, right?"

She thought about it. "Must be. Strange. And I'm in my house. I wonder how much time has passed there."

"Who knows. Could be minutes, could be hours. Surely not more than a night or my grandmother would have barged in and woken me."

"So it's like we're dreaming there?"

"Something like that." Theo glanced at her shoulder. "You must have entered the game before I did, though."

"Why do you say that?" she asked.

"Your bars ran out before mine."

"Oh." She lifted her sleeve to reveal clear, unmarked skin. The bars were gone. She stared at the spot for a moment before saying, "Thank you. You saved me."

Heat warmed Theo's cheeks once again. "Of course. I couldn't leave you—I mean, Leah …" He furrowed his brow. "Why'd you choose the name Leah?"

She shrugged. "It's what my friends call me now. I don't know … I think it sounds more grown-up than Annelee."

"I've always liked your name."

"Really?"

Theo mimicked her shrug. "Really."

She quickly turned away, but not before he saw her grin. "Did you see this?"

A waist-high pedestal stood in the center of the Waystation. An aged book lay open on top.

"A book." Theo joined her. "I'm supposed to find a book in the game."

"Me too. Do you think this is it?"

Theo fingers grazed the yellowed paper. "I don't think so."

"Yeah, I guess that would be too easy."

Theo checked the front cover for a title. When he found none, he flipped back to the pages that had been left open. "I'd completely forgotten about finding a book, just like Talya said I would."

Annelee nodded. "Rescue Princess Rosaline, save the Kingdom of Viren, and find a book." She shook her head. "I forgot all of it. How in the world are we supposed to beat this game if while we're inside it we can't remember anything Talya said?"

Theo pointed to the open book. "Maybe this will explain. Look. It's a letter from Talya."

"Read it," she said. "Aloud."

Theo straightened his shoulders and drew a deep breath. "Dear Dream Travelers …"

"Dream Travelers!" She gripped his arm. "Remember when I came up with that name?"

"I remember." Memories filled Theo's mind. "We were in Mrs. Baily's class, about a week after we returned from Other Earth with the second seal."

She looked surprised. "You do remember."

Theo held her stare. "Of course, I do. I remember everything about you."

Annelee bit her lip to fight back a smile, then returned her gaze to the book. "Keep reading."

"Right." Theo's eyes scanned the text. "Dear Dream Travelers, I hope you're enjoying this little quest I've crafted for you. By now you've discovered each other's presence in the game. Good. I'm happy to have reunited the two of you. You make a good team."

"We do make a good team," Annelee interjected.

Theo continued. "As I already explained, you won't see me again until you discover your true purpose. To do that, you must rescue the princess, save the Kingdom of Viren, and find a book. And no, not this book."

Annelee chuckled and shook her head.

"As a reminder, I created this game because you've forgotten the truth of who you are." Theo paused and glanced at Annelee. "You forgot too?"

Her gaze drifted past Theo. A faraway expression formed on her face. "I guess so." Her eyes slowly found his. "I mean, I must have. Because I'm not even sure what Talya means when he says I've forgotten who I am."

"Yeah," Theo said. "Me either."

She tapped the page. "Go on."

He continued reading. "In these pages you'll find the basic rules to help you navigate the next level of the game. Congratulations on reaching this milestone. However, do not celebrate your victory too soon. Though this is a game, much is at stake. Lose your Life Bars here, and you'll remain stuck in the game. Worse, if you fail to recall who you are, I'm afraid you may never remember."

Annelee shifted.

Theo pointed to the page and read Talya's final words. "That's all for now, Dream Travelers. Stay focused on your mission; choose love over fear; and above all, remember who you are. Godspeed. Talya."

Theo turned the page to the game rules and instructions. He cleared his throat and read through the bulleted list. "First: choose your avatar, then select your avatar's third item."

"Oh yeah, I remember Talya saying we'd get to pick our avatars sometime."

Theo moved on to the next bullet point. "After selecting your avatar, enter the charging station to refill your Life Bars for the next level of the game."

Annelee pointed to the white door in the protruding wall across from them. "There," she said.

Theo nodded. "Reminders: inside the game, you'll have five bars indicating how much time you have left before you need to reach the next Waystation. Life Bars fade as time passes and as you use your avatar's skills. As your skills grow stronger, your Life Bars fade faster."

"Maybe that's why my bars faded faster than yours."

"Maybe." Theo paused. "This next part is in all caps."

Annelee looked over his shoulder and read it aloud. "DON'T LET YOUR LIFE BARS RUN OUT." She swallowed. "Good thing you were there to save me."

"Yeah." Theo took a deep breath. "Good thing." He pointed to the page. "Last one: 'Remember, whatever you did as your previous avatar is now a part of the game's history. You won't recall details from that time, but you will remember emotions.'"

"So I won't remember that you saved me?"

"I guess not."

"But I'll remember how I felt about you saving me? How does that work?"

"I don't know," Theo said. "I guess you'll remember our …" He wanted to say *connection*. Instead, he said, "Friendship."

She folded her arms across her chest. "Hmm … Maybe that's why I was drawn to you from the beginning."

"You were?"

She nodded. "You know what's funny? Your avatar sort of looked like you, but I didn't recognize you. Did

11

my avatar look like me?"

"Maybe a little," Theo said. "Your hair was darker, but your eyes were the same."

"Interesting."

"Well, that's it." Theo closed the book. "Those are the rules."

Annelee's eyebrows darted up. "Then let's go pick our avatars," she said with a mischievous grin.

He followed her to the Waystation's command center, where she tapped one of the screens. A stylized image of Annelee appeared, dressed in the same tank top and jeans she now wore. She swiped her finger, and her appearance changed, matching the image Theo knew as Leah the herbalist.

"That's my last avatar." She swiped again to see the next option. "Farmer's daughter? No thank you."

Theo watched her scroll through several options before stopping on one. "Lady of the court. Hmmm … That could be interesting."

"I wouldn't want to be anywhere near the palace of Viren after what we just saw."

"Good point." She swiped again. "Oh! This one—archer!"

Theo leaned in to examine the avatar: a fit young woman with raven-black hair cut short into a choppy bob. She gripped a bow in her right hand and wore tan leather pants tucked into tall boots. A red long-sleeved shirt peeked out from her leather vest, and a long billowy cloak draped her shoulders.

Annelee tapped her finger on the screen, then used the keypad on the counter to type.

"What are you doing?" Theo asked.

Her cheeks flushed pink. "Changing my avatar's name."

The name *Annelee* appeared on the screen.

"Not Leah?" he asked playfully.

She ignored him. "Look. My avatar comes with a bow and a quiver of arrows. Now I get to pick my extra item."

Theo stepped to the next screen. "I'm going over here to pick my avatar." He touched the screen to start, then started swiping. He scrolled through several options before pausing on the warrior.

Avatar Backstory: a fourteen-year-old boy, citizen of Viren, who began training with the King's Guard two months before Marsuuv arrived. Now a member of the rebellion who fled with Sir William Atwood. Parents Reid and Louisa were killed by Dark Riders in a recent raid on the city.

Theo looked away from the screen, wondering why—if he was going to forget—Talya placed so many painful reminders in the game.

"Maybe that's the point," he said under his breath.

"What was that?"

"Nothing."

Theo noted his avatar's attire: tan leather from head to toe, like Annelee's character, but in his hands, he gripped a sword and a shield. He tapped a button that said Avatar Abilities and read the details aloud. "Strength, speed, and swordsmanship." He shrugged. "Seems pretty basic for a warrior."

"Oh cool," Annelee said excitedly. "My backstory says I'm a recent recruit in the King's Guard, and now I'm a member of the rebels."

Theo confirmed his avatar selection. "Me too. Maybe we'll know each other from the start this time."

"Maybe! What did you pick for your third item?"

He scrolled through the options, then tapped the hunting knife. "I'll go with the knife." He confirmed his choice.

"That's what I had as the herbalist. I picked the journal and quill this time."

Theo furrowed his brow. "Why?"

She flashed a playful grin. "I'm going to use it to write things down … So we can remember."

Theo glanced back at his selection. "Good idea."

"Yeah, I got the idea from my previous avatar. I mean, having a journal was helpful the first time around."

"I wish I would have thought of that. But I think it's too late for me to—"

"C'mon!" She grabbed his arm and pulled him toward the charging station. "I'm dying to see what's inside."

Theo joined her and stood directly in front of the white door, noting again the intricate filigree carved into the wood. He glanced up at the large circular shield that hung above it, eyes tracing the thin white line that encircled the green band, then the vibrant red cross. Finally he pulled his attention to the tiny white dot in the center. It appeared to glow against the other colors.

"Look!" Theo pointed.

The shield came to life with an energetic hum, illuminating the five components of the design with a neon glow.

Theo touched his chest, feeling warmth spread through his body. His mind stirred with hazy memories.

"A seal," he said. "Five seals."

"White," Annelee said, wonder filling her voice. "Green, black, red, and white … From Other Earth." She paused. "I'd forgotten about the seals." She turned from the shield to look at Theo. "I can't remember what they mean."

"Me either."

"I *wish* I could remember."

Theo nodded. "Me too."

A gentle click pulled their attention to the white door. It slid open, retracting into the curved wall.

"I guess it's time to recharge," Annelee said, peering into the dark room on the other side.

Theo stared past her. "Ladies first," he said.

Annelee rolled her eyes. "Still afraid of the dark?" She chuckled and walked past him through the doorway. Theo smiled as he followed her inside.

The door slid closed behind them, sealing out all light.

"Now what?" Theo asked.

"Look!"

A white medallion came to life in the center of the black floor, pulsing with a soft glow. It cast just enough light to see the interior of the charging station, which was the size of a large closet.

"It matches the shield above the door," Annelee said, pointing to the red bars that intersected the white dot and reached wall to wall. Green and white bands encircled the walls in two even stripes of color. "C'mon." She grabbed Theo's hand and pulled him toward the center.

"What are we doing?"

"Don't you feel it?"

"Feel what?" he asked.

"Shhh … Listen."

Theo stilled his whirling mind and focused on the hum. And then he felt it—a gentle pull on his body, drawing him toward the white center.

"It's calling to us."

It sounded strange when she said it, but Theo knew exactly what she meant.

With their fingers still interlocked, Theo stepped onto the medallion, pulling Annelee with him.

Light burst through the floor as their feet connected with the circle.

Annelee gasped.

A rush of energy shot through Theo's body, waking every cell of his being. The shock pushed the air from his lungs in a sigh of wonder. A tingle formed in his bones, reminding him of the sensations he'd felt as the bard whenever he used the gift of his voice. But this time, the sensation consumed him. Soon he forgot Annelee's presence. He barely felt the warmth of her hand in his.

The tingle spread through Theo's body, energizing him with light. Then it settled in his mind, unlocking his memory.

Images unfolded in rapid succession.

A desert wilderness, a lion made of sand, green waters, and a boy with bright blue eyes.

A dusty, hidden room in a library, a drop of blood, and a starburst of light.

Friendship, belonging, and love.

Five seals of color and light.

White, green, black, red, and white.

The Five Seals of Truth.

"Elyon," Theo whispered.

A soft giggle echoed through the room.

And then Theo remembered everything.

Love poured over him and filled him. A sob burst from his lips.

He dropped to his knees on the white medallion, pressing his palms against its warm, humming surface. Annelee was already there, weeping.

The surge of light and love intensified, pulsing through every fiber of Theo's being. It seared his body like flames of a fire, yet never consumed him. It burned, and yet he couldn't get enough.

Memories of Theo's father came next, their conversations from the days following Theo's return from Other Earth.

"I'm proud of you," his father had said.

"You inspire me."

"I love you."

Bottled grief flowed freely—tears Theo had needed to shed for months but couldn't. Now he let it out in great heaving sobs as the love of Elyon penetrated his heart.

And this time he heard the words spoken in the boy's voice.

I'm proud of you.

You inspire me.

I love you.

Heat seared Theo's right shoulder. He sat up and opened his eyes to see the Five Seals of Truth branded on his skin with glowing light.

Set me as a seal upon your heart, as a seal upon your arm.

The boy's voice resonated in his mind.

"White," Theo said. "Elyon is the infinite light. In him there is no darkness. Nothing can threaten him, and nothing can threaten us, because we are the children of Elyon."

Annelee sat up beside him. "Green: We are the light of the world. Black: Our journey is to see the light in the darkness." She continued. "Red: Surrender is the means of seeing the light."

"And white," Theo concluded. "True love is the evidence of being in the light."

A voice echoed through the charging station like an exclamation mark on their declarations.

Remember!

As the sound of the voice faded, Theo placed his palm over the seal on his arm, wondering how he could possibly forget.

Chapter Two

THE LIGHT SLOWLY FADED, and Theo rose to his feet. Annelee joined him a moment later, tears streaking her cheeks. Neither of them spoke for several seconds, but their eyes communicated everything.

"Wow," Annelee said.

"Yeah, wow."

"How … how could I have forgotten something so … I mean, it's …"

"I know," Theo said. "It's everything."

"It's the *only* thing."

Theo nodded, then sighed. He glanced around the room. "Look." He pointed to a black door. "Was that there before?"

Annelee shook her head. "I don't think so."

A soft glow outlined its rectangular frame. A second later, a button appeared on the door with the words *Re-Enter Game* flashing in gold letters.

"Black," Theo said. "The door is black. You know why, right?"

"Blindness," Annelee responded. "As soon as we leave this room, we're going to forget everything." She chewed her lip while staring at the door. "I don't want to leave." She grabbed Theo's hand and faced him. "I don't want to forget again."

His mind raced. He didn't want to forget either. "We won't this time. We just have to remember."

"But that's the thing; we *won't* remember. It's part of the game."

"Yes, but there *must* be a way to remember. That's also part of the game. We have to remember who we are."

"I remember now," Annelee said, touching her arm.

"Yeah," Theo's fingers grazed the tattoolike seals on his own arm. They pulsed with light.

"My journal," Annelee said. "When I came out of the Waystation the first time, I had a few seconds when I could remember everything—my real life and my avatar's life. Maybe that will happen again. I'll write it all down."

Theo nodded. "Are you ready?"

"No," Annelee said, her voice filled with regret. "I'd stay here forever if I could."

"Me too, and we can. We can have this feeling forever—these memories forever—*if* we win the game."

"Right," she breathed. "Then I guess I'm ready."

Still clinging to Annelee's fingers, he took a step forward, raised a tentative hand, and touched the re-entry button.

A glowing number three flashed on the door, then a two.

Remember, a voice whispered.

A number one blinked bright on the door then disappeared, taking every ounce of light with it.

A soft hum resonated in Theo's ears, then intensified. The floor of the Waystation rumbled beneath their feet. And then the entire building vanished, replaced by a starry night sky.

Annelee immediately released Theo's hand, yanked a satchel from her shoulder, pushed up her sleeves, and began digging through its contents.

"I have to write things down," she said. "We have to—"

"Remember," Theo finished her sentence. "I know."

He stared at her, distracted by her appearance. Though her avatar was the same age as Annelee, she looked older, harder. Muscles rippled in her forearms as she pulled the journal from her satchel. She met his stare with a relieved smile. Though her cheekbones were higher, her hair dark as night, and her skin the color of someone who spent hours outdoors, her eyes remained the same.

He wondered how he looked to her.

Theo wandered a few steps away. "It's crazy … I can remember everything right now." He pushed up the sleeve of his shirt, seeing that five Life Bars now replaced the Five Seals of Truth. "I remember my name, my life in Florida. I remember that I'm in a game and that my last avatar was a bard." He scanned his surroundings, seeing two horses tied to trees at the edge of the clearing. "I remember the backstory of my new avatar. I remember when we tied up those horses so we could recharge, but I also remember carrying you through the woods, as the bard, because your Life Bars ran …"

Theo stopped midsentence.

An ache pounded in his head, clouding his thoughts. He kneaded his temples, waiting for the pain to pass. When it did, he turned to see his comrade Annelee kneeling on the ground, hunched over a journal, quill in hand over the page as if caught in midthought.

She glanced up at him, shook her head as if waking from a trance, then stood. "Theo." She scanned him head to toe. "What … what are we doing out here?"

"Replenishing our life force, remember?"

Confusion etched her face for only a moment before clarity dawned. "Blast this curse from Marsuuv!" She slammed her journal closed. "If not for this hex, we wouldn't have to sneak around." She scanned the clearing. "Sir William will find out if we're not careful."

"Maybe that's not such a bad thing," Theo said, touching the hilt of his sword at his waist. "Perhaps we should come clean and tell him the truth."

"Are you insane? He'd disavow us! Marsuuv is his sworn enemy. If William knew we bore the markings of that beast, he'd never permit us to be members of his army—rebellion or King's Guard. Our careers would be over before they began. Or worse."

The look on her face told Theo the conversation was over.

"Do you think there are others?" he asked.

"Others? What do you mean?"

"Others who've been cursed as we have."

"Oh. I hadn't considered it." She paused. "But surely there must be …" Her voice trailed off. Questions lingered in her silence. Finally she said, "Why us? Why has Marsuuv marked us?"

Theo shook his head. "I've been wondering the exact same thing. But maybe it wasn't Marsuuv."

"Then who?" she asked.

He shrugged. "Who knows. Just a thought." He gestured to her journal. "What were you writing?"

Annelee flipped open the leather booklet and scanned the pages.

She started to read aloud. "Remember the Five Seals …" She paused, scanned the text, then said, "None of this makes sense. There's a list of colors, something about blood and Shataiki … I don't even know what that word means. It's all gibberish." She closed the journal, returned it to her bag, then touched a hand to her temple. "I have a headache."

"Me too. We should probably get back to camp. Based on Elijah's timeline, William and the others should have returned from the palace by now."

"If they were successful," Annelee added.

"If …" Theo repeated. "You know, I hadn't considered they might fail. We should have gone with them. Instead they took the bard and the herbalist."

Annelee stared west. "William had his reasons. Let's get back to the cave and find out what happened in our absence."

Theo led them across the clearing to their horses. Several quail strung on a thick cord draped the withers of his mare.

"I'd nearly forgotten how many quail I shot," Annelee said. "Do you think it'll be enough to convince them we've been out hunting all night?"

"I doubt it. We'll have to come up with a better excuse to explain our delay." He mounted his horse. "C'mon, we can work on our story as we travel."

He watched Annelee check the five bars on her right shoulder. A faraway look formed on her face as she traced a finger over the lines. She tugged her sleeve back into place, mounted her horse, then faced Theo. "You saved me." Gratitude filled her voice. "I … Without you, I would have run out of bars and died. Thank you."

Theo pushed up his sleeve, showing her his own markings. "We're in this together," he said. "We may have been cursed by Marsuuv, but that doesn't mean we must live as cursed beings. Together, we'll find a way to our freedom. I promise." He pulled his sleeve back into place. "Let's go."

Annelee nodded, snapped the reins of her horse, and took the lead through the dense forest.

Theo followed close behind, eyes fixed on her back, wondering how he would ever manage to keep his promise.

Chapter Three

THEY ARRIVED AT THE WATERFALL midmorning the next day. Theo led the way under the thundering water, whistled, and waited for a reply. A few seconds later, a second whistle replied from the darkness of the cave.

Once inside the main cavern of their camp, Theo caught sight of William and his men. They sat around the fire, shoulders hunched, and heads bowed together as if in deep conversation. Elijah glanced up first, noticed Theo and Annelee, then waved them over to join. But before they could cross to the center of the cave, Eloise intercepted Annelee.

"Hello, dear," she said while wiping her hands on her apron. Relief filled her voice. "You had me worried. You were supposed to be back yesterday evening."

"Hi, Mom." Annelee wrapped the woman in a hug. "We got caught up."

Eloise pulled away and eyed Theo suspiciously.

He handed her the quail. "For dinner."

"And what kind of situation would require the two of you to get caught up in the forest all night?"

"Dark Riders," Theo explained. "Thankfully we saw them before they saw us. We had to take a longer route back to camp." He nodded his head toward William. "Now if you don't mind, our commander wishes to see us."

"Of course," Eloise said. "I'm glad you're both safe." She patted her daughter's cheek, then returned to the kitchen area with the quail.

"Wolf! Hawk!" Liam stood and motioned for Theo and Annelee.

"Will he never tire of these nicknames?" Annelee groaned.

"I suppose not," Theo said, though he didn't mind being referred to as a skilled canine hunter. Wolf. The nickname had a ring to it. Surely Liam could have come up with something far worse to call him, like worm or maggot.

William stood as they joined and offered each of them his forearm in a familiar greeting. Theo clasped the prince's arm, then took his seat.

"Where have you been?" William asked.

"Hunting," Theo said.

"All night?"

Annelee offered the explanation this time. "We nearly ran straight into a patrol of Dark Riders combing the forest. We had to hunker down to wait them out, then take the long route back to camp."

"I'm not surprised," Liam said, returning to his seat. "Surely we stirred them up during our narrow escape from the city."

"So the plan failed?" Theo asked. "Did the white lilies not work as the herbalist thought they would?"

William shook his head. "The antidote seemed to have worked. But Marsuuv's hold on the king is far too strong. He didn't just poison the king, he's bound himself to Tyrus with some kind of dark power."

"Speaking of the herbalist …" Annelee said. "Where is she?" She glanced around the cave.

"And the bard." Theo said. "Elijah said they both went with you."

William exchanged silent glances with his men. "We lost them."

"You lost them?" Theo asked.

William sighed. "We were separated." The prince's eyes flicked back and forth as if rewatching the events in his memory. "Marsuuv … He was there." William shook his head. "He was more interested in killing the bard than me. None of it makes any sense."

A shiver ran down Theo's spine at the mention of Marsuuv.

"We waited for them at the white pine," Conrad explained. "We waited as long as we could. We only returned to the caves shortly before the two of you arrived."

Elijah hung his head. "The bard wasn't the most pleasant boy, but I would never wish him harm."

Liam kicked one of the logs. Sparks flew up toward the dim cave ceiling. "We have to do something, or they won't be the only ones who die!"

"What do you mean?" Annelee asked.

Conrad shifted. "We saw the prisoners in the dungeon. They're set to be executed a week from yesterday."

Fury welled inside Theo. "We have to do something!"

Conrad placed a hand on Theo's shoulder, but Theo shoved it away. "This monster, Marsuuv, is responsible for the deaths of my parents! I will not sit back and allow him to inflict this pain on other families."

Annelee watched him from across the fire, hands clenched together in her lap. Redness tinged her eyes, and Theo knew she was thinking of her own father, who'd also been killed in the raids.

"I know your passion for the cause," William said. "Don't forget that this monster has stolen someone precious from me as well." He turned his attention to Conrad. "Which brings me to my next concern. The guard we apprehended at the palace said Rosaline is rumored to be with Marsuuv's master. The Roush in the Dark Forest made mention of him—Teeleh, I believe. The Roush said he's confined to the Dark Forest. So if Rosaline's with him, that's where we'll find her." He paused, holding Conrad's stare. "I want to return to the Dark Forest."

"Absolutely not," Conrad said.

"What's a Roush?" Annelee asked.

"Not now, Hawk," Liam cut in.

"I am your prince," William said, attention still fixed on Conrad.

"You are my *soon-to-be* prince," Conrad corrected. "And I am your second-in-command."

"Precisely," William jabbed back. "Therefore, you will do as I say."

"You placed me in this role for a reason," Conrad said. "Because you know I won't blindly follow your every command. This is a fool's mission, and I won't condone it."

"Remember what the herbalist said about human blood. It's poison to Shataiki. We can use this knowledge to defend ourselves and attack Teeleh's minions!"

Theo saw Annelee straighten her shoulders.

"Shataiki? What's a Shataiki?" When no one answered her, she took out her journal and began flipping through the pages.

"We have no guarantee the blood will work," Conrad argued. "Look what happened with the white lilies and the king." He shifted and leaned forward. "William, I understand you love Rosaline. But you need to think with your head and not with your heart. When you marry her, you'll be the prince of Viren. Which means you're responsible not just for Rosaline's safety but the entire kingdom."

"He's right," Elijah said. "So long as we keep you alive, your betrothal to her remains in effect, and Rosaline is free from marrying that monster. We *will* rescue her, but first we must liberate those Marsuuv has imprisoned. We can't do that if our leader is shredded to ribbons by Shataiki talons."

The word *Shataiki* felt familiar to Theo, and not just because he'd heard it in passing from Annelee's ramblings in her journal.

The muscles in William's jaw clenched. He tugged at his hair in frustration. "I know you're right," he said. "But I can't bear the thought of her being with that beast for one more second. We need a plan."

Feeling bold, Theo straightened his shoulders and said, "Whether we choose to storm the Dark Forest or advance upon the city to rescue the prisoners, we need an army."

"Do you think we're unaware of our measly numbers?" Elijah scoffed. "Where in all of Viren do you suggest we find this army?"

"Not in Viren," Theo said. "In Saxum. We should seek help from the north."

Liam burst into laughter. "You must be joking."

"I'm not. We could just—"

"No," Conrad interrupted. "It's forbidden to enter another kingdom's territory. Besides, the people of Saxum are barbaric. You've heard the tales. They'd kill us on sight."

William stared into the flames as if lost in a trance. "I read something interesting about the Kingdom of Saxum. The herbalist's father wrote about the land in his journal."

Conrad groaned. "You can't be serious."

"What did it say?" Liam asked, shifting his tone.

"Not you too," Elijah said. "Conrad, talk some sense into them."

"Just listen." William stood and paced. "Wolf has a point."

"He's fourteen!" Elijah interjected.

William turned on him. "He may be fourteen, but he has the instincts of a warrior twice his age." He shook a finger in the air. "No, I think he's on to something."

"Your love for Rosaline is clouding your judgment," Conrad said.

William ignored him. "The herbalist's father had filled his journal with details about the Dark Forest, but there was a small section with notes of other excursions, one of them to Saxum."

"What did it say?" Theo asked.

"Don't encourage him!"

William held up a hand to silence Elijah. "Years ago, her father traveled to Saxum in search of a rare desert plant. His description of the northern people was nothing like the rumors of barbarians."

"Are we going to trust the diary of a crazed old man? Again?" Elijah added. "I mean, he was wrong about the lilies."

"He wasn't wrong about the lilies," William said. "They did work for a time. We're simply up against a much more powerful force."

"What else did the herbalist's father say about Saxum?" Theo asked.

William dipped his head. "Three things that lead me to be optimistic about your suggestion to seek their help."

"Go on," Conrad said, his tone shifting to one of interest.

William continued. "During his time in the

northern kingdom, the daughter of the king of Saxum fell gravely ill. Through his knowledge of plants, the herbalist's father saved her life."

Conrad nodded. "We can use that to build rapport."

"Exactly," William said. "The journal also detailed a conversation between the herbalist's father and King Joseph, the ruler of Saxum. He said the king openly discussed a change that was coming." William paused dramatically. "The king wanted to unite the kingdoms of Saxum and Viren."

"And the third thing?" Theo asked.

A smile spread across William's face. "They have a large army."

Theo returned the grin.

"Well done, Wolf," William said. "Without a doubt, it's a risky plan. But it's the only plan we have." He stood and faced his men. "Refresh yourselves and prepare to leave after we eat."

Elijah folded his arms over his chest. "I want to note that I still think this is a terrible idea."

William smirked. "Noted."

Theo stood to his feet. "Let us come with you."

William hesitated before saying, "Look, I appreciate you both as members of this rebellion, but neither of you have completed your training. And this will be a dangerous mission."

"Yes, of course," Theo said. "But you know my

skills with a sword and hers with a bow." He pointed to Annelee. "We could be useful."

"He's got a point," Elijah said. "Maybe they should come."

"You?" William said with shock. "*You* think they should come?"

Elijah shrugged. "They're young and naïve, but as you said, they're skilled beyond their years. And fearless—a blessing and a curse at their young age."

William looked Theo up and down, then scanned Annelee. "Fine. Wolf and Hawk will join us." He walked away and called over his shoulder. "Pack your things and say your good-byes. Let's hope your presence on this mission *is* a blessing and not a curse."

Theo and Annelee stood, watching as William and his men dispersed through the cave to prepare for their trip north. Theo touched the hilt of his sword. The cool metal sent a shock through his fingertips and up his arm, reminding him of the five black bars hidden beneath his sleeve.

"Let's go," he said to Annelee, trying to ignore the fact that their presence already was a curse.

Chapter Four

ANNELEE SHIFTED in the saddle. Sweat rolled down her back, and her pants clung to her legs. She longed for a sleeveless shirt but knew that wouldn't be an option anytime soon. She tried unsuccessfully to ignore the subtle crawling sensation beneath her skin where the five bars marked her right shoulder, wondering if her skin actually itched or if the mere thought of the marks made her arm tickle. She shifted her focus to the changing scenery.

Nearly an hour had passed since they crossed from the deep-green forests of Viren into the craggy, mountainous terrain of the northern Kingdom of Saxum. Without the shade of the dense trees, the midday sun beat down on the rebels, making the already tense journey even more stressful. Annelee had felt the angst the moment they left the caves yesterday afternoon. By the time they'd made camp for the night, the entire rebel group was on high alert. And after another half day's ride, Annelee could feel her insides tensing like a bowstring. A glance over at Theo suggested he felt the same. He caught her staring.

Annelee looked away.

She fixed her eyes straight ahead on the red-and-orange-streaked rock formations that jutted from the dry earth. After several long seconds, she dared another glance at Theo from the corner of her eye.

He sat tall atop his horse, one hand on the reins, the other resting lightly on the hilt of his sword. His ever-watchful eyes scanned the terrain as he rode. Sunlight highlighted his golden hair and deepened the bronze of his tan skin. Annelee's eyes traced the cut of his jawline. He looked so different now, more like a man than the boy she'd grown up with.

They'd lived on the same cobblestone street since the age of three, attended the same school, and began their training for the King's Guard during the same season. She'd known Theo for most of her life, but now, in the setting of the rebel army, he seemed different: older, wiser, and even more adept with his sword. He'd certainly earned the nickname Wolf, though she couldn't bring herself to call him that.

The sound of his voice interrupted her thoughts. "Look!" Theo pointed straight ahead.

Annelee followed his finger to see a lone goat between two towering megalithic stones. The horned animal turned to stare at them, blinked its enormous eyes, then lowered its head to munch on some scraggly desert weeds.

"We must be nearly there," William said. "Stay close."

Elijah nudged his horse toward Annelee's to tighten up their formation. "We're breaking the highest law of every territory," he mumbled. "They'll have every right to shoot us on sight."

Two more goats appeared in the distance. Then three more.

"Surely there are shepherds nearby," Conrad said. "Keep your eyes open. And remember, give them no reason to see us as a threat. We come in peace."

Annelee nodded but touched her bow. Its presence calmed her nerves.

They rounded another boulder and entered a small canyon. A dozen or so goats peered down at them from the cliffsides. Their tiny hooves balanced on impossibly thin ledges of stone. Annelee watched, mesmerized, as the horned animals scaled the rocks with ease, loosing tiny pebbles as they leaped from foothold to foothold.

A scream jolted her from the trance.

She jerked her horse to a stop. In front of her, William, Liam, and Conrad did the same. Elijah and

Theo pulled up on either side of her.

The scream came again, echoing toward them from somewhere deeper in the canyon.

Annelee's blood ran cold.

When she heard the scream a third time, she reacted without thought, snapped the reins of her horse, and took off at a gallop.

"Hawk!" William called after her. "Annelee, stop!"

But she ignored her commander, instead listening to the voice of instinct inside her own mind.

The voice that told her this was no ordinary scream.

The shriek came again, and this time Annelee could tell it was a child—a young girl in distress. The shrill sound echoed through the canyon and awakened every warrior cell in Annelee's body. With a tingling surge of energy, she pushed her horse forward, faster.

The sound of racing hooves pounded behind her. Seconds later, William and Theo closed in on either side.

"Stop!" William shouted. "I command you to stop!"

Again, Annelee ignored him.

William tried to reach for her reins. "You're going to get us killed!"

Feeling a warm swell of energy pulse through her body, she dug her heels into the horse's sides, pressing the animal to unleash whatever speed and strength it had.

The canyon twisted left as Annelee pulled away from her fellow rebels. Her eyes scanned the scene. About fifty feet up on the cliff wall, two little girls cowered on a small overhang of rock. Another thirty feet or so above them and to the right, a shepherd peered down over the ledge. And between them, navigating a thin shelf of stone, a mountain lion prowled, its eyes fixed on the young girls.

The shepherd shouted to the girls in an unfamiliar language. Despite the language barrier, Annelee could hear the fear in the girls' voices as they yelled back.

Their predicament was clear—the shepherd couldn't reach them.

Annelee jerked hard on the reins, but before the horse could even stop, she leaped from its back and drew her bow, propelled by the fiery energy that surged through her arms and legs. She sprinted toward the girls, shutting out the roars of her teammates as they commanded her to stop.

Her trained eyes scanned the canyon floor, searching for the perfect vantage point. They landed on a two-foot-high boulder twenty yards from where she stood. She took off in a sprint, drawing an arrow from her quiver as she ran. Closing in on her target, Annelee nocked the arrow, jumped, and tucked, flipping up and onto the boulder. A wave of power jolted through the soles of her feet as her boots hit the mark. The warm quivering force settled in her arms as she drew back on the bowstring, took aim, and began counting.

Five.

She sucked in a deep breath.

Four.

Calculated the distance.

Three.

Took note of the wind.

Two.

Noticed the coil of muscle in the cat's haunches.

One.

She exhaled and released the arrow.

The sound of the bowstring reverberated in her ear.

The arrow sailed at least a hundred and fifty yards, not streaking toward the spot where the cat was, but to where Annelee knew the animal would be. The mountain lion leaped into the air at the exact moment she anticipated, paws outstretched, swiping at the young girls. The powerful body of the animal soared from one rocky ledge to the next.

Five feet from where the girls cowered, the arrow sank into the mountain lion's side, directly behind its front leg. The cat slumped, collapsing on the edge of the overhang directly in front of the children.

The girls gawked at the mountain lion, then slowly turned to look at Annelee. She lowered her bow, nodded to the girls, then met the eyes of the shepherd who stared at her from the ledge of the cliff.

Seconds later, Annelee's friends surrounded her.

The sound of horses' hooves filled the canyon. Dust clouds rolled over the top of the cliff. The shepherd disappeared only to return a moment later. A dozen men on horseback appeared beside him, each with a drawn bow. Their arrows pointed directly at Annelee.

"So much for not giving them a reason to see us as a threat," Conrad mumbled.

Annelee glanced at Theo. His eyes told her everything she needed to know: regardless of what happened next, Annelee was right to save the girls.

She nodded her head at him, sucked in a deep breath, then raised her hands in surrender.

Chapter Five

THEO FOLLOWED ANNELEE, his wrists bound with a thick abrasive cord. Ahead of them trudged William and the other rebels, also bound. Two of the Saxum shepherds rode at the front of their little caravan while four others flanked it, two on each side. The remainder of the shepherds trailed in the back along with the two young girls, the rebels' horses, and their weapons. Theo touched his bounds hands to his left hip, feeling naked without his sword.

The midday sun beat down on them, making the hike across the mountainous, arid earth even more grueling. Thankfully, the ground sloped ahead of them, granting Theo and the other warriors reprieve from the rolling landscape. He steadied his footing on the uneven earth and began the descent. Loose pebbles rolled under his boots as he trekked down a steep incline. The terrain transformed as they entered a wide basin.

Trees and other greenery sprang up from the earth, contrasting against the reds and oranges of the rocky world. A deep-blue lake became visible through the trees, surrounded by a few dozen tent structures. Towering rock formations rose from the earth like chimneys, some of them connected to one another with swinging rope bridges. Theo hoped they weren't about to be led across one of them.

After another thirty minutes of travel, they finally reached the bottom of the basin. The temperature felt at least fifteen degrees cooler in the center of the oasis. A few men and women exited their tents as they passed, staring at the group of strangers. The distinct smell of goats reached Theo's nostrils, and a moment later they passed an enclosure with at least thirty of the horned creatures. Their captors led them past the lake, where children drawing water peered up from their task, whispering and pointing. Theo noted the goatskins they wore.

Finally the caravan stopped. Theo peered around them to see a large permanent tent dwelling of at least three rooms. Another goat pen sat to the left of the canvas structure. The animals stared at the rebels through slats in the fence, their jaws moving side to side as they chewed.

A man dressed in animal skins stormed out from

the main entrance of the tent. His sun-darkened skin contrasted against the crisp white headcloth he wore.

"Father!" One of the little girls ran from the back of the caravan to hug the stern-looking man.

He draped an arm around the girl, who couldn't have been more than nine years old, then stroked his dark beard.

"What's the meaning of this?" he asked in the common tongue, as if he wanted the rebels to understand. "Who are these intruders and why have you brought them to my doorstep? You know the rules: it's forbidden to enter another's kingdom." His eyes landed on William.

The lead shepherd dismounted. "Forgive me, Abraham." The man dipped his head. "But your daughter insisted I bring them before you."

"My daughter is but a child. Do you take your orders from children now?"

"No, sir, but—"

"I tried to tell him, sir." Another rider dismounted, adjusting a brown headcloth. "I told him we had every right to kill them on the spot."

"Father!" The girl tugged at his arm.

"Not now, Rebecca."

She ignored him. "That girl saved my life." She pointed a finger at Annelee.

The man called Abraham paused, glancing down at his daughter.

"She saved Chloe and me from a mountain lion."

Abraham turned his attention to Annelee. "Is this true?"

The lead shepherd answered. "It's true. I might not believe it if I hadn't seen it with my own eyes. It wasn't an easy shot—near impossible, in fact. We're lucky she was there. From where I stood at the cliff's edge, I couldn't have hit it."

Abraham fixed the other shepherd with a severe stare. "Ethan, you knew about this and still suggested their deaths? Have you no respect for our customs? I owe these people a debt." He faced the rebel warriors. "If I don't fulfill it, I could invite misfortune upon my home."

The shepherd removed his brown headcloth. "Please forgive me, Abraham. I was only trying to protect our land. We can't be too careful these days."

Abraham paused as if considering his words. "You're forgiven. Now please, unbind my guests."

A few of the other shepherds dismounted to help release the rebels.

"And please refresh their horses," Abraham added. "I will take over from here."

The shepherds dispersed, leading the horses around

the side of the tent to a large barnlike structure behind the goat pen.

Abraham faced Annelee. "Thank you," he said, "for saving my daughter. Though, I must ask, how did you become so skilled with a bow at such a young age?"

Theo detected the subtle sadness that flickered across Annelee's face. No one else would have noticed it. "My father taught me," she said.

"He must be proud to have a daughter like you."

"*Was* proud," Annelee corrected. "He's recently deceased."

"My apologies." Abraham dipped his head. "Please allow me to repay my debt by offering you a meal." He turned with young Rebecca in tow and entered the tent.

Theo sat cross-legged on a goatskin in front of a low wooden table. Annelee reclined to his right, Liam to his left. William, Conrad, and Elijah took their places across from them. A moment later, Abraham joined at the head of the table.

"My wife was already preparing the evening stew," he said. "It'll be ready shortly. In the meantime …" He gestured to his daughter, Rebecca, who entered with a large clay carafe. She walked around the table and began filling wooden cups with a thick white liquid.

"Milk?" Theo asked. He hadn't had milk since fleeing the city.

Abraham nodded. "The finest goat's milk in all of Saxum. Please, enjoy."

Theo took a sip of the smooth, sweet drink.

"Now," Abraham shifted at the head of the table. "Why is it you've come here?" He rested his hands in his lap. "Had you not saved my daughter, Ethan would've been within his rights to do with you as he pleased. You're either fools or desperate. So which is it?"

William set down his milk. "We come from Viren," he said. "And we seek audience with your king."

Abraham smiled softly. "I believe you mean *queen*. Our beloved king passed from this life to the next a mere six months ago. His daughter is our chief now."

"His daughter?" William asked. "Did he not have a son to assume the throne?"

Theo saw Annelee roll her eyes.

"It's our custom for the eldest child to assume the throne," Abraham said. "Trust me, Queen Naomi is a capable and worthy ruler."

Annelee smiled.

"Forgive me," William said.

Abraham nodded. "Rebecca, please refill our guests' beverages, then you may serve the stew."

The young girl appeared at Theo's side to top off his

drink. She mumbled under her breath. "Thank Elyon it was Queen Naomi who took the throne and not Cain. He's a monster."

"Elyon?" Theo said to her, but before she could answer, Abraham cut her off.

"Rebecca." He shot her a stern look.

"What?" Rebecca said, moving to refill Annelee's cup. "It's true! He seeks to lead a rebellion against his own sister and bring war to our land."

"Daughter …" Abraham's tone held a warning.

She ignored him. "He's dangerous! He's polluted the minds of too many of our people, even my own brother Steffos."

"Hush, child!" Abraham commanded. "Mind your tongue."

Rebecca huffed.

Abraham fixed her with his stare. "Please serve the stew."

Rebecca bit her lip, then retreated to the back room.

Abraham stroked his thick black beard. "I apologize for my daughter's loose tongue. She's young and passionate and misses her brother dearly."

William straightened his shoulders before speaking. "I gather that Cain is the late king's son? And Steffos—your son—has left to join him in rebellion against the queen?"

Abraham paused as if deciding how much to reveal.

Finally he sighed and said, "Yes. I'm afraid so. Cain's actions have devastated our entire community. Even my own household."

"So you don't align with Cain's cause, then?" Theo asked.

Elijah glared at him from across the table. "Drink your milk, and keep your mouth shut."

"No, he's fine," Abraham said. "You're right, boy. I don't align with Cain—nor my son. My loyalties lie with the queen. It has caused a great division in my family."

The flap to the main entrance of the tent swept open. Daylight streamed in, backlighting a shepherd in the doorway. Theo recognized him as the leader who had brought them here.

"Abraham, I'm sorry to interrupt, but five Defectors have just arrived in the village …" The man paused and glanced at the rebels. He dropped his voice. "Led by your son."

Abraham slowly stood. "Very well. You may send him in."

The shepherd nodded, then ducked out of the tent.

"Defectors?" Theo asked.

Abraham straightened his shoulders and fixed his stare on the doorway. "Yes, Defectors—Cain's riders." Lines creased his forehead. "If there were time, I would hide you, but I'm afraid we don't have that luxury."

The tone in his voice unsettled Theo.

A moment later, a young man burst into the tent with two others behind him. Dressed in black goatskins, they darkened the doorway with their presence.

"Son," Abraham said in greeting.

Steffos stepped forward. Thick stubble lined his chiseled cheeks, and tattoos decorated the shaved sides of his head. He wore the center strip of hair long and pulled back into a braid. "Father," he said in a harsh tone.

The men on either side of him stepped farther into the tent. Black paint lined their faces.

Steffos's dark eyes scanned the room. He spat. "I had to see it for myself, but it seems the rumor was no lie."

Abraham stepped toward him. "Welcome, my son. Would you like something to eat?"

"You expect me to eat with these outsiders?" Steffos asked. "How dare you allow them refuge in our home?"

Abraham straightened. "Last time I checked, this was still *my* home. You're the one who no longer lives here." He fixed his son with his stare. "So you heard I have guests, but did you also hear that they saved your sister's life?"

Steffos's body tensed, but his jaw relaxed.

Before he could respond, Rebecca reappeared, carrying a large pot. Her eyes lit up, and she quickly set the stew onto the table. "Steffos, you're back!" Theo noticed the way the girl started to run to him, then caught herself. She stood at a distance. "I can't believe it. You've returned."

"No, sister," he said, in a tone much softer than what he used with his father. "I have not returned. I've come to collect the outsiders."

"Collect them?" Abraham asked.

"Yes." Steffos's face hardened once again. "I'm taking them to Cain."

Abraham shook his head. "I cannot allow you to do that. I owe these people a debt. You know the importance of this custom."

"An *old* custom," Steffos said in a mocking tone. "An old custom enforced by an old man. A man, I might add, who no longer reigns in this land. When Cain finally takes the throne, there'll be a new way of doing things in Saxum."

Abraham nodded. "And until then, I will honor the queen who *does* sit upon the throne. Again, I owe these people a debt for saving your sister's life. Does that mean nothing to you?"

Steffos looked to his sister, then at the rebels. "They can't stay here," he said to his father. "What do you intend to do with them?"

Abraham folded his hands at his waist. "I plan to offer them a meal, shelter for the night, then return them to their land in the morning."

Theo started to protest, wanting to insist that they must see the queen, but Annelee grabbed him by the forearm. He pressed his lips together and settled in his seat.

"How do I know you'll do as you say?" Steffos asked.

"Do you distrust me that much, son?"

Steffos cocked his head. The men on either side of him crossed their arms over their chests. "They can sleep in the barn with the other animals," Steffos finally said. "My men and I will make camp here for the night to ensure they leave at dawn." He turned on his heel and swept open the tent to leave. The two other Defectors followed him out without a word.

"Steffos!" Rebecca called after him.

Abraham placed a hand on her shoulder. "He's lost, child—for now."

Tears streaked the girl's cheeks.

William stood. "I'm sorry for the additional tension we've brought upon your family, but we can't leave without speaking to your queen."

Abraham brushed his hands against his pants, then returned to his seat. "I'll discuss this no further. Please finish your meal, and I'll have someone show you to the barn for the night."

Rebecca wiped her eyes, then picked up the pot of stew. Without speaking, she made her way around the table, filling each bowl with the hot meal. When she stopped to fill Theo's, she wouldn't even look at him. Desperation lingered on her face as she ladled the hot food, then retreated from the tent.

Theo caught Annelee staring at him as he dipped a wooden spoon into the stew. They exchanged looks, and he knew she was thinking the same thing he was. It seemed Viren wasn't the only kingdom under the oppression of a dark ruler.

Chapter Six

THEO LAY ON HIS BACK on a stack of straw, staring up at the rafters of the barn. The musky stench of goats lingered in the air. His eyes drifted to a small window in the far wall where stars glittered in the nighttime sky.

"So what's the plan?" Liam asked.

Theo rolled onto his side to see one of his fellow rebels a few feet away, seated on a hay bale.

"What do you mean?" Elijah asked. "We sleep, then travel back to Viren in the morning. What else can we do?"

"No, Liam's right," Conrad said. He paced through the barn. "We can't go back to Viren. We must speak to the queen. We need the support of Saxum and its army if we're to face off with Marsuuv and free the prisoners he's detained. We need to leave now."

"There are shepherds everywhere," Elijah protested,

sitting up from where he lay. "They might as well be soldiers. We also have no idea where to find the queen. Saxum is a massive kingdom."

Annelee wandered over to join them from where she'd been rummaging through some of the barn's tools and supplies. "We're also running low on rations. We've only a couple days before we'll need to restock. And Saxum isn't exactly a bustling kingdom. It's going to be tough to find what we need."

Theo sat up. "So what do we do, William? Leave now in search of the queen?"

William waved his question away. "I need to think." He crossed over to the window and peered out. Theo noted the creases in his brow. They seemed too deep for a man in his twenties. He knew the disappearance of Rosaline weighed on him—and more and more every day.

The barn door burst open, startling the goats.

Abraham entered, carrying a lantern and stack of blankets. He scanned the group of rebels, then quietly closed the door. "Please listen to me carefully, and keep your voices down."

William stepped away from the window.

Abraham's chest rose as he sucked in a deep breath. "I overheard my son and his men speaking. They have no intention of allowing you to return to your kingdom in the morning. They've already sent word to Cain's camp and arranged for more Defectors to join them here to collect you. Elyon only knows what they'll do to you then."

Theo shifted on the straw. The man's words stirred something in his mind.

"I don't agree with Cain's ways and his unnecessary bloodshed," Abraham continued. "So I'll do everything in my power to keep you alive. But to do so, we must leave now. I'll sneak you out through the back fields and escort you to the border of Viren to ensure your safety."

"We can't go back yet," Theo interjected.

William held up a hand to silence him. "I'll handle this, Wolf." William stepped toward Abraham. "He's right. We can't return to Viren without speaking to your queen. Our beloved kingdom is in grave danger. We must see her."

Abraham searched William's face. He shook his head. "I can't allow it. I'm sorry."

William lowered his voice. "Please," he said. "Surely you know the pains of seeing your kingdom ripped apart."

Abraham stared at him for a long moment. "The path to the statehouse is dangerous."

"So be it," William said. "We have no other choice.

We must speak to the queen."

Abraham stroked his beard. "Fine. I'll take you to Queen Naomi, but please know that I can't guarantee your safety."

He lifted the top blanket off the stack in his arms, revealing several waxed-cloth packages that contained food and other provisions.

"Please put these in your packs," he said. "We leave now."

Early morning sunlight warmed the red-gold landscape of dirt and rock. Theo nudged his horse forward. William and the other rebels rode ahead of him, following Abraham. Annelee's horse trotted beside his.

Hours had passed since they fled under the cover of darkness, following Abraham across the back fields of his property. They'd collected their horses along the way, leading them quietly until they were far enough from the sleepy village where Abraham and his people dwelled. As soon as they'd been certain Steffos and his men weren't following them, they mounted the horses and raced north toward the Saxum capital.

Now it stretched before them, a large city made of simple adobe structures. The geometric buildings lined either side of the dirt road they traveled. A woman stood outside one of the houses, hanging wet clothes on a line to dry in the morning sun. Outside another house, a young boy tended a small garden while his mother kneaded a ball of dough, then placed it inside the outdoor adobe oven.

"What's with all the goats?" Annelee leaned over and asked Theo. She pointed to the horned animals that walked the city streets.

Theo shook his head. "It must be one of the kingdom's primary resources."

They followed Abraham deeper into the capital as the city began to awaken. Twenty minutes later they passed vendors and what looked to be a school.

After a few minutes, a sprawling white building appeared on the horizon. Wood pergolas and arbors connected at least a dozen individual modules.

"Whoa," Annelee said. "It's a whole compound."

"More like a palace," Theo said. "This has to be Queen Naomi's house."

Abraham led them toward the expansive structure and into a white-walled courtyard.

Rust-colored bricks paved the ground, and surprisingly lush green plants sprang up from the garden beds. The sound of a bubbling fountain reached his ears. In the midst of a desert kingdom, this home had all the markings of royalty.

The courtyard path wound around a giant stone

structure and led to a brightly painted red door. Two men stood on either side, dressed similarly to the shepherds of Abraham's village, but on their wrists and ankles they wore thick bands of gold. They stared at the approaching caravan with severe expressions.

Abraham held up a hand, and William pulled his horse to a stop. The other rebels did the same, watching as Abraham dismounted and handed his horse's reins to William. He adjusted his headcloth, then approached the men at the door.

From where Theo watched, he couldn't hear what Abraham said, but he could see the way their host gestured with his hands as he spoke, pointing to the rebel crew. The guards whispered to one another and nodded.

Abraham rejoined William. "My debt to you is paid." He took the reins from William. "Good luck."

"You're leaving us?" Theo asked.

"This is *your* battle for *your* kingdom. I have my own to deal with." He mounted his horse and trotted away.

One of the guards approached William. He said nothing but held out an open palm. William dismounted, then handed his horse over to the palace guard. He gestured to the other rebels to do the same. The guard at the door motioned for them to follow him inside the house.

Cool air greeted them along with the sweet scent of baking bread. Theo followed his fellow warriors as they were led down a long white hall. The same rust-colored bricks covered the floors, and dark timbers spanned the ceiling. Giant ornate vases lined both walls, spaced out every ten feet or so. Theo's fingers grazed one of them as they passed.

Annelee shot him a look.

"What?" Theo whispered.

She shook her head. "I've got a bad feeling about this whole situation, and you're not helping. You're going to break something."

Theo smirked but held her stare. When they passed the next vase, he touched it too.

"Theo!" she said in a loud whisper and swatted his arm.

William glanced back and shot them a look.

"Fine," Theo said and looked away, but his smile lingered. He loved when Annelee called him by his name.

The guard stopped when they reached an arched doorway at the end of the hall. "Wait here." He entered and returned a moment later, motioning for them to follow.

The room opened into a massive circular chamber. Windows lined one side like a half-moon, allowing golden morning light to warm the stark space. A white stone platform sat opposite the openings; both it and the throne it held were made from the same adobe material. A copper-colored goatskin draped the seat.

"Please take a knee for Queen Naomi," the guard said.

William obliged, and the other rebels followed his lead. The hard stone floor dug into Theo's knee.

A woman entered from an arched door in the wall behind the throne. She moved silently, feet bare, body draped in a flowing white gown. The fabric contrasted with the rich brown of her skin. Delicate bracelets dangled from her wrists and ankles. Five gold bands adorned her long neck, their designs mimicking the ornate headpiece that draped her forehead just beneath the pile of gold fabric that wrapped her hair.

She narrowed her deep-brown eyes and pursed her full lips as she took her seat upon the throne, crossing one long leg over the other.

Two women entered from the same door, dressed in plain tan smocks and simple gold jewelry—lady's maids, Theo guessed. They took their places on either side of their queen.

William dipped his chin and touched his forehead. "Queen Naomi. Thank you for seeing us."

"You may stand," she said in a deep, rich voice. "What is your name?"

William rose to his feet. Theo and the other rebels did the same. "I am Sir William Atwood, future prince of the Kingdom of Viren, next in line to the throne, and betrothed to Rosaline, King Tyrus's daughter."

Queen Naomi's lips flickered with a smirk. "Well Sir William Atwood, future prince of Viren, next in line to the throne, betrothed to Rosaline. What is it you seek? I heard you were desperate to speak to me, so speak." She folded her thin arms over her chest.

"Yes, of course. I'll get straight to the point. We come to you in great need. An evil stranger from the Dark Forest, Marsuuv, has overtaken our land. He's poisoned the king's mind, kidnapped my betrothed, and turned our once vibrant kingdom into a land of shadows."

Theo noticed the way Queen Naomi's face flinched ever so slightly at the mention of Marsuuv.

"And what concern is this to me?" she asked.

William straightened his shoulders. "If Marsuuv can do this to our kingdom, he could surely do it here."

She cut him with her eyes. "Are you suggesting Viren is superior to Saxum?"

"I mean no offense, Your Highness. But I've watched a single man with no weapons walk into my kingdom and destroy it in mere weeks. Only these warriors you see here and a small number of others have managed to escape his clutches."

She stared at him, unimpressed.

William shifted on his feet. "Many years ago, an herbalist named Marlowe entered your kingdom."

A look of surprise flickered on Queen Naomi's face. "How do you know this?"

"I knew his daughter, Leah," William said. "She too was an herbalist and was recently killed by Marsuuv."

Queen Naomi furrowed her brow. "That is unfortunate. But I still don't see what this has to do with me or my kingdom."

William hesitated, then took a small step toward her. "I read Marlowe's journal. I know he saved your life."

She tilted her head.

"I also know that your father, King Joseph, shared with Marlowe his vision for a united Viren and Saxum. So what does this have to do with you? Well, I stand before you today, hoping you are your father's daughter …" He paused. "And not your father's son."

Naomi's nostrils flared. "You speak of things you know nothing about."

William held up his hands in defense. "Again, I don't mean to offend. But I'm a desperate man running out of options. Perhaps if I could prove to you how dangerous Marsuuv—"

She held up a hand to cut him off. "I already know of Marsuuv. I do not need to be warned of his danger."

"You know him?" William said.

Naomi waved an elegant hand through the air. "Of course I know him. Who else do you think poisoned my brother's mind against me?"

William took another step forward. "Then you know he must be stopped."

"I do." Queen Naomi uncrossed her legs and stood. "It's unfortunate that Viren is facing the same treachery as Saxum. But I still don't understand. What do you want with me and my kingdom?"

William hesitated. "We seek the assistance of your army. As I said, our rebellion is small—no more than twenty warriors. We don't stand a chance against Marsuuv and his Dark Riders. But with your vast and powerful army—"

"So it's bloodshed you want then?"

William shook his head. "No. Viren is my home. Its people are my people. They've been deceived by Marsuuv. I'd never wish to harm them. My plan is a show of force. And with your army, we'd easily outnumber them. Marsuuv will have no choice but to consider surrender. His blood is the only blood I intend to shed."

Naomi paced in front of the throne. "So you want my army." She paused. "But what advantage is that for my people?"

"I thought it was obvious," William said. "We have a

common enemy. Together, we can destroy him."

She lifted her chin. "I appreciate the offer, but I don't need your help. I can save my brother—and my kingdom—all on my own."

"I believed the same thing about my king," William said. "But I failed and nearly got everyone with me killed." He gestured to his warriors.

Naomi stepped down from the white platform and crossed the room to the windows. She pushed back a sheer curtain and gazed out at her kingdom. "I've always known my brother envied me for being the first-born. I suspect Marsuuv had to do very little to turn Cain against me. He's taken this rivalry much further than I ever would've imagined, severing our beloved Saxum in two. Even without a war, the division could destroy us. But if my brother has his way, there will surely be a war."

She turned back to William. "I can't give you my army. I need them here to protect my people."

"I understand," William said. "And I'm sorry to hear you find yourself in a similar predicament. But if we cut off the head of the snake together, it can no longer strike and poison our people—yours or mine. Help me destroy the man who's deceiving your brother before he turns on your kingdom."

She stared at him for a long moment, then pushed away from the window and returned to her throne.

"You need my army only as a show of force? That is your plan? You assure me there is no risk to my people?"

William approached the throne, dropped to a knee, and placed his right hand over his heart. "Dear Queen, I assure you, I have no intentions to spill the blood of my people or allow harm to come to yours."

Naomi gracefully took her seat, draping her arms over the sides of the throne. "You've given me much to think about." She lifted a hand and snapped her fingers. "Guards, please take our guests to protective quarters while I give all of this some thought."

Annelee paced the library where Queen Naomi's guards had confined her and the other rebels. Thankfully, the staff had provided refreshments during their long wait. Now, with full bellies, both Liam and Elijah reclined on linen couches, dozing. William and Conrad sat on the far end of the room, staring out the window while engaged in quiet conversation. The soft murmur of their voices drifted through the library.

Annelee crossed to the opposite side of the room where Theo sat cross-legged on the floor, eyes closed, leaning his head against one of the bookcases. Annelee tapped his boot with hers. He opened his eyes.

"Were you asleep?"

"No," Theo mumbled. "Just thinking."

Annelee took a seat beside him. "About what?"

Theo glanced around the vast library, his eyes scanning the rows of books that lined the walls. "I was wondering how long it would take all of the goats in Saxum to eat every book in this library."

Annelee grinned and drew her knees to her chest. Her shoulder brushed against Theo's. "Not long, I suspect. There must be at least five goats for every book."

Theo smirked. "Do you think they get tired of it?" he asked.

"Of what?"

He gestured to the serving tray the palace staff had brought them. "Goat cheese, goat milk, goat meat, goat pastries …"

"Goat pastries?" Annelee wrinkled her nose.

Theo chuckled. "I made it up. But if anyone has goat pastries, it's the people of Saxum."

Annelee laughed with him. From the couch, Liam cracked open his eyes, squinted at them, then winked. Heat flushed Annelee's cheeks. She lowered her voice and leaned even closer to Theo, feeling the warmth of his arm against hers, touching the spot where her curse was hidden. She tried not to think about how many bars she had left.

"Would you eat a goat pastry?" she asked him.

Theo made a face like he was thinking. "It depends …"

"On?"

"On whether or not *you'd* eat a goat pastry. I mean, I'd eat one if you did. Would you?"

Despite their attempts to continue the playful banter, Annelee couldn't shove away the thoughts of Marsuuv and the marks he'd left on her arm. She cast a quick glance at Liam, whose eyes were closed once again, then quickly took note of Elijah, William, and Conrad. No one paid attention to her or Theo.

She reached into her satchel and pulled out her journal. Pressing a hand against the smooth leather cover, she asked in the faintest whisper, "How many bars do you have left?"

Theo's smile faded. He scanned the room, then leaned away from her and discreetly lifted his sleeve. He pushed it back down and whispered, "Three. You?"

Annelee pressed her lips together. "I checked about an hour ago, when the guard escorted me to the facilities." She turned and held his stare. "I only have two."

"Two?" Theo whispered. "That doesn't make any sense. We recharged together. How's that possible?"

Annelee flipped open her journal and scanned the smeared words on the page. Beneath the cryptic note about Shataiki blood—which inexplicably matched

a theory the herbalist had shared with William—
Annelee had written her own theory. One she wasn't yet
ready to share with Theo. She glanced up from the page
and stared at the bookshelves that lined the library. A
strange sense of déjà vu washed over her. "I don't know.
But there's something else …"

"What?"

"These books," she said. "I can't explain it, but there's
just something about them."

Theo shifted. "Like you need one of them, right?" he
asked. "Or a book somewhere. Like it's calling to you."

She met Theo's stare.

"I know what you mean," he added. "Because I've
been thinking the same thing."

Before Annelee could respond, she heard the library
door click open. One of the guards walked in. "Queen
Naomi wishes to see you," he said. "She's reached her
decision."

Chapter Seven

LATE MORNING SUNLIGHT streamed through the throne room windows and warmed Theo's shoulders as he took a knee before Queen Naomi. William and Annelee bowed on either side of him; Conrad, Elijah, and Liam flanked their leader. The queen motioned for them to rise.

She crossed her legs and leaned back. "You're an honorable man, Sir William Atwood. The Kingdom of Viren would be lucky to have you as its ruler."

Theo noted the way she said *would be*.

"I, too, would do anything for my land and its people. Which is why I can't give you my army. Despite your assurances, there is still a risk of bloodshed, and I won't place my people in harm's way. It pains me to send you away empty-handed, but I have no regrets."

William rushed forward. "But Your Highness—"

Two guards quickly stepped in front of him, blocking

his approach to Queen Naomi. Each goatskin-clad man gripped one of William's arms.

"My decision is final," Naomi said, unfazed. "My guards will escort you from my palace and back to your border."

The guards who held William pulled him back from the throne.

Theo opened his mouth to protest as well, but a boisterous voice filled the room.

"Sister! How are you?"

Theo snapped his head to the left to see a man leaning against the arched doorway. An elaborate patchwork vest of black and gray goatskins clad his thick torso. The muscles of his arms flexed as he pushed away from the door and sauntered into the room. He paused before Naomi, standing inside a shaft of light cast by one of the open windows. The golden beams warmed his dark-brown skin.

A quick glance between the two siblings, and Theo could see the family resemblance. "Cain," he whispered.

Footfalls filled the chamber as a dozen Defectors marched in after him, Steffos in the lead.

Cain casually ran a hand over his shaven head. "It's rude to ignore a greeting." He extended both arms toward Naomi. "Come now, Sis, let's have a hug," he said in a playful tone.

A chill ran down Theo's back. Annelee stepped closer to him.

Queen Naomi didn't flinch. "Cain, what are you doing here?"

"Can't a brother visit his sister?" he asked, still speaking in mock pleasantry.

"You haven't darkened my doorway in over a month," Naomi said. "So tell me, *Brother*. What is it you want?"

Cain chuckled and began to pace in front of the throne. "You're right." He paused and pointed at her. "Though, I did miss you." He raised his eyebrows, then resumed his pacing. "I heard you had visitors, and I couldn't resist the opportunity to meet them."

Cain faced the rebels and scanned them with dark eyes. "Welcome to the Kingdom of Saxum." His smile morphed into a sneer.

Theo couldn't be sure, but he thought the man's stare lingered longest on him.

Naomi sighed as if bored by Cain's antics. "Very well, you've made your point. Now please leave us." She waved a hand toward the door.

"Now, now," Cain said, turning back toward her. "This is my land too. I have every right to know their intentions in my kingdom. Especially when we have clear treaties with the Kingdom of Viren regarding each other's borders and boundaries." He glanced over his shoulder at William. "Agreements that have now been violated."

"They seek an alliance with the army of Saxum," Naomi said. "*My* army. They seek our assistance to rescue King Tyrus, who's been poisoned." She pierced Cain with her stare. "It appears Marsuuv's influence has spread beyond Saxum's borders."

Cain continued his charade. "Dear Sister, the problem is that you still see Marsuuv as a threat, when in reality he's our redeemer. *Our savior*. What he offers is far greater than any prosperity our kingdom has ever experienced. But you're too blind to see it."

Naomi shook her head. "No, what I'm too blind to see is how one man could've deceived you so easily and deeply. I still don't understand how you've fallen under his spell."

Cain lowered his voice. "He's not just *one man*."

Theo took a small step back.

"Now, I insist you allow me to take these intruders off your hands." Cain nodded at the rebels. "You'll give me at least that much."

"I will do no such thing," Naomi said. "And their business here is finished. They were just leaving. Guards, please escort my guests to their horses and to the border."

"I'll return them to the border," Cain said, a smile

in his voice. "No need to busy your guards with such a menial task. My men and I are headed in that direction anyway."

Theo couldn't miss the bitter rivalry between the brother and sister. He and the others were merely pawns now.

"I doubt it," Naomi said. "And no. You'll kill them."

"It's my right!" Cain snapped, then composed himself. "They're trespassing."

Naomi waved a hand through the air. "Guards, please remove my brother and his men from my home."

The two men who'd previously been holding William released him and approached Cain. He towered over them. "Fine!" With little effort, Cain slapped their arms away. "Then I invoke Duellum Mortis."

A look of shock crossed the guards' faces. The lady's maids gasped.

Keeping his voice low, Theo leaned toward Annelee and asked, "What's that?"

She shrugged.

Naomi calmy answered, "Duellum Mortis is an outdated custom that we haven't used for decades." Raising her eyebrows, she said, "It's a tad barbaric, Brother, even for you."

"It's been invoked for far lesser offenses," Cain

said, stepping away from Naomi's guards. "Besides, I thought you loved our father's old traditions."

Naomi narrowed her eyes.

Cain paced the room once again, this time speaking loudly, as if making a decree to the entire throne room, perhaps even to the entire Kingdom of Saxum. "Once invoked, Duellum Mortis must be carried out." He made a fist with his right hand and pounded it over his heart. "I, Cain, Son of King Joseph, Prince of Saxum, invoke the tradition of Duellum Mortis against these outsiders." He paced in front of the rebels, stopping to stare each one in the eye. "To be carried out this very night," he added.

"Your Highness, I hate to interrupt," William said. "But seeing as this involves me and my warriors, I must ask, what is this *Mortis* business?"

Standing in front of Elijah, Cain turned to face William. He slowly stepped toward him, then walked straight past to pause in front of Theo. He narrowed his eyes and answered as if Theo had asked the question. "It's a test of strength in which two people enter an arena and only one leaves. A duel to the death," he added with a sly smile.

"Fine." Queen Naomi interrupted the awkward conversation.

Theo exhaled as Cain turned to face her once again.

Naomi rose from her seat. "You will have your Duellum Mortis. Now, name your conditions."

Cain gave a playful bow. "Ladies first, dear Sister."

Silence lingered in the wake of his words. Naomi's lips twitched as she locked eyes with her brother. Though her expression remained unchanging, Theo felt as if he could see the inner workings of her mind as she carefully calculated the situation and formulated a plan.

She stood, scanning the rebels as she stepped down from the platform. "As you wish. First, I will be Viren's sponsor, and if my champion wins"—she paused dramatically and turned to face Cain—"not only will I escort our guests back to their land, but I'll also send my army with them to defeat this Marsuuv you seem so enamored with."

Theo saw the muscles in Cain's jaw tick.

"What?" Naomi asked, feigning her own surprise. "Do my conditions not work for you, Brother? We can always cancel the duel and find a more civilized way to handle this."

Cain shook his head. "No." He straightened his shoulders. "Very well. Your conditions will stand. Now, here are mine." He turned to face the rebels. Once again, his stare landed on Theo. He pointed a finger.

"This boy will be your fighter."

Theo felt the blood drain from his face. Annelee grabbed his forearm.

"Absolutely not!" William objected. "He's just a boy. I will represent the people of Viren in this barbaric practice—I and no one else!"

Both Naomi and Cain ignored him.

Cain continued, "And when my champion wins, these trespassers shall be mine to do as I wish with them."

"Are you so afraid to challenge these men that you must choose the only boy among them?" Naomi asked. "I'm surprised you didn't pick the girl."

"Hey!" Annelee objected.

Cain held up a hand to silence her. She pressed her lips together.

"Those are my conditions," Cain said to his sister. "I've accepted yours. Will you not accept mine?"

Her golden-brown eyes narrowed with intensity. "Agreed. But why the intense interest in these strangers? You take a huge risk."

Cain looked at Theo and scoffed. "Not especially huge."

William rushed the queen and grabbed her arm. "Queen Naomi, I must insist—"

The guards yanked him away.

Naomi nodded to them, and they loosened their grips. "Sir William, I'm afraid once the conditions have been proposed, they cannot be revoked." She paused. "Though neither you nor I understand the true reason for them."

William swore under his breath.

Cain clapped his hands together. "We have a duel then! How exciting!"

Theo's thoughts swirled. "So I'll be fighting Cain?" The question slipped from his mouth without conscious thought. He scanned all six feet four inches of muscle that was the Prince of Saxum. He tried to swallow against the dryness in his throat.

"Who? Me?" Cain touched a hand to his chest. "Oh no. I'm the prince. I don't fight. I have my own champion to handle my battles for me." White teeth gleamed against his dark skin. He lifted his hands to the sky. "Bring in Lahmi!"

An ashen color washed over Queen Naomi's face.

Theo's stomach plummeted.

He turned to watch the Defectors part just inside the doorway.

Annelee's fingernails dug into his arm as they watched a beast of a man duck his head to enter the throne room.

"Oh my …" Annelee's voice drifted off.

Theo stumbled back into her, staring at the seven-foot-tall man.

"Rebels of Viren!" Cain declared. "Meet Lahmi, my champion!"

Chapter Eight

ALONE IN A DARK STONE TUNNEL, Theo peered through the iron gate that separated him from the roaring crowd—and Cain's champion, Lahmi. Pillars of fire flickered in the night and illuminated the packed circular stadium. He wiped his sweaty palms on the front of his pants, trying to calm the stampede of nerves in his gut. The tension had been slowly building throughout the day as he awaited his fate in the Duellum Mortis. Now he felt as if he was about to throw up.

After Cain had challenged Theo, Naomi's guards dragged an outraged William from the throne room and placed him in a prison cell to settle down. The other rebels had been escorted back to the library while Theo was placed in a private room attached to the stadium. Naomi's guards had brought him food and drink, but the only thing he could stomach was the water. Left with his own thoughts until the death duel, Theo couldn't help but think of the marks on his arm. The fact that he, of all the rebels, had been chosen to fight a literal giant only proved that he *was* cursed. Which didn't bode well for the outcome of the fight. He hadn't bothered looking at the bars again, realizing it no longer mattered how many he had left.

Tonight, Theo would die.

No more than thirty minutes ago, two of Naomi's guards had escorted him from the waiting room through a locked wooden door and into the corridor where he now stood. The guards had told him he would not be allowed to bring his own weapons. Everything Theo would need he'd find inside the stadium.

Peering through the gate, his eyes scanned the dirt fighting ring. Torchlight glinted off four large metal chests that sat at each of the four cardinal points. One lay just ahead of Theo, no more than twenty feet past the gate.

"The weapons have to be in there," he muttered. "Okay," he sighed. "I can do this. I can do this."

The click of a lock echoed in the tunnel behind him. He turned, seeing two figures silhouetted in the doorway.

"Five minutes," a male voice said.

"Thank you." Theo recognized Annelee's voice.

A moment later, she appeared beside him, firelight illuminating her face. She remained expressionless as she reached out and touched his forearm. But Theo saw the terror in her eyes.

"Annelee …"

She silenced him with a hug, squeezing him tighter than anyone had ever hugged him before. She buried her face against his chest, and for a long moment, neither of them spoke. Both of them allowed the warmth of their embrace to communicate the emotions that words never could.

Theo ran a hand over her short black hair, then finally asked, "How'd you get in here?"

Annelee pulled away and glanced up at him. "I appealed to the queen. I only have a few minutes." Her hands lingered on his arms. "How are you doing? I mean … How are you holding up?"

Theo swallowed and cast a glance over his shoulder. Annelee followed his gaze. "I guess as well as anyone who's about to be ripped apart by a giant could."

She reached up and turned his face toward hers, allowing her fingers to linger on his cheek. "You can't talk like that. Yes, your opponent is …"

"Massive."

"Yes. Massive. But you're fast and good with a sword—the best I've ever seen, in fact. Plus, you have unrivaled instincts." She trailed her fingers across his jawline, then placed her hand on his chest over his heart. "War is as much a mental game as a physical one. You have to believe that you *can* win." She chewed her lip. Tears pooled in her eyes, but she didn't allow them to spill over. "You have to come back to me," she whispered.

Theo nodded.

"Say it. Say you'll come back to me."

"I'll come back to you."

She nodded, dropped her hand from his chest, then cleared her throat. "Now listen closely to what I'm about to tell you. I'm almost out of time." She didn't wait for him to respond. "I have a theory." She pulled up her sleeve to reveal two full bars and three empty outlines. "Ever since we compared our markings in the library, I can't stop wondering why I have one less than you. I also can't stop thinking about that arrow I shot yesterday when I saved those girls. I mean, I'm a good shot but not that good. It's as if I willed the arrow into its target."

"What are you getting at?" Theo asked, hearing the roar of the crowd swell.

She pulled her journal from her satchel and flipped it open. "I know this sounds crazy, but what if they're connected?"

Theo shook his head, not understanding.

"What if the curse Marsuuv put on us has a side effect—one he doesn't even know about?"

"Like what?" Theo asked.

"What if it makes us stronger, more skilled? Like I said, I shouldn't have been able to hit that mountain lion. No one should have, and yet I did." Her finger grazed the words on the page. "Look at what I wrote here: 'What if our skills are connected to our life force?'"

"That doesn't make sense. Your father taught you well, that's all. Why would Marsuuv curse us with something that made us stronger? It makes no sense at all."

"None of this makes sense, Theo!" She snapped the journal closed, then composed herself, stuffing the little leather booklet back into her bag. She stepped closer to him, her face a breath away from his. "Look. I know it sounds crazy. I get that. It's just a theory, but it's the only one we have. And if it's real, you can use it to your advantage." She lowered her voice. "Maybe while you still have strong life force, you're capable of a strength you don't even know you have. Just like me."

Theo searched her face. "Annelee, I—"

"No." She pressed her fingers to his lips to silence him. "I need to believe your life force can save you. I need to believe it even if it isn't true."

Theo wrapped his fingers around her hand, pulled it away from his lips, then slowly brought it back. He kissed the tips of her fingers.

The door clicked open behind them. "Time's up!"

Annelee held his stare for one last second. "Come back to me," she said as she turned and walked away, disappearing behind the door as the guard closed it.

Once again, Theo was alone.

Her words raced through his mind.

Maybe you're capable of strength you don't even know you have.

He allowed his mind to linger on the thought.

The roar of the audience escalated into a wild frenzy. Theo wrapped his fingers around the bars of the gate and peered through. A man stood in the center of the stadium floor, waving a flag with the Saxum crest. A moment later, he stepped out of view. The gate rumbled in Theo's hands. He released it, watching it swing open.

The cheers of the audience faded to the background. Theo stepped through the gate into the stadium and scanned the silent crowd. He had to get to one of the metal chests where he would presumably find weapons.

But before he could move, Lahmi entered the arena across from him. Bare-chested with a goatskin kilt, the man appeared ten times more fearsome than he had in the throne room. Tattoos covered his bulging biceps.

Twitching muscles lined his tree-trunk-sized legs. A single braid emerged from the top of his shaven head and reached to his shoulder blades. The giant pounded his chest and released a beastly howl.

Ice formed in Theo's veins. He quickly scanned the crowd, taking note of where the rebels sat directly below Queen Naomi's viewing box. Annelee shuffled past William, then took her seat. Theo looked away and sucked in a sharp breath. He pushed it out and drew another, filling his lungs with air.

Queen Naomi stood and raised her hands, silencing the crowd. The deafening quiet pulsed in Theo's ears. The sound of his own heartbeat shattered the hush. Torchlight warmed Naomi's face and glimmered off her golden jewelry as she locked gazes with the flagman. He lifted a goat-horn trumpet to his lips and waited.

The queen turned her face toward Lahmi and nodded, then shifted her focus to Theo. She held his stare for what felt like an eternity, then gave him a slow nod. In one swift motion, she dropped her hands. The flagman blew into the horn, filling the arena with a deep, resonant tone.

Theo moved swiftly, racing to the nearest chest. With each footstep, he pushed thoughts from his mind.

No more Annelee. No more rebels. No more

Marsuuv. No thoughts of his parents, their brutal deaths, or his own grief. And no more theories about curses, strengths, and life forces.

The only thing that mattered now was Theo and Lahmi.

And the fact that only one of them would walk away from this fight.

Theo threw open the chest of weapons, eyes scanning his options. Clubs, staffs, and battle hammers. He allowed his instincts to take over and reached inside.

A warm buzz raced through his palm as his hand connected with a thick piece of hardwood. He yanked out a six-foot-long warrior's staff. A jolt of energy pulsed up his arms as he locked both hands around the wood and turned, drawing the staff back in a semicircle. A glance across the stadium revealed that Lahmi had already selected his weapon from one of the chests as well —a spiked mace. He hefted the iron ball, gave it a test swing, then locked eyes with Theo.

Raising the weapon above his head, Theo released a wolflike howl, then slammed the end of the staff into the dirt. He blinked, sure that he saw rings of light ripple out from the spot where the staff contacted the ground. The earth beneath his feet trembled.

A warm thrum pulsed up Theo's legs. Letting go of his final thoughts about his life, his mortality, and the outcome of the duel, Theo took off in a sprint, staff at his side.

Lahmi rushed him with a battle cry. Before they met at the center, the giant was already swinging his mace.

Theo jumped to the left, dodging the blow. As his feet hit the ground, he propelled himself back into the air, circling his staff overhead. He brought it down hard, putting the full force of his body weight behind the strike. But Lahmi was quick and blocked Theo's staff with his forearm.

A loud crack resonated through the stadium. Theo backed away, caught off guard as Lahmi laughed. He'd easily shrugged off a blow that should have broken his arm.

Clearing his mind, Theo once again forced his awareness into his body. He struck the air with his staff, feeling the movements flow like water. Though he'd trained with a staff, it had never been Theo's weapon of choice. But now the instrument moved as if it were an extension of his body, as if it were the only weapon he'd ever known.

Gripping the staff in one hand, Theo executed a handspring with the other, followed by a backflip. Landing in a crouched position, he locked eyes with Lahmi, then charged. Closing quickly, Theo leaped into the air and spun, striking Lahmi with his foot and staff at the same time. The giant stumbled to one side but regained his footing.

With an infuriated roar, the man attacked.

His mace connected with Theo's staff, nearly tearing it from Theo's grip. Again the man struck, and again Theo deflected the mace. Then again.

Theo's body moved with a speed and agility he'd never experienced, not even when he was in the heat of training with the King's Guard back in Viren.

When Lahmi paused his attack, surely wondering how a smaller opponent was able to thwart his blows, Theo leaped into the air and slammed the butt of his staff into the giant's chest. The impact reverberated through the staff, up Theo's arms, and straight into his head.

Images flashed through his mind.

Giant black bats.

Red eyes.

Sharp fangs.

Theo stumbled, caught off guard by the beastly images. They seemed so real. His body pulsed with memories of having fought them with a staff like this one.

Déjà vu washed over him. He shook his head.

Lahmi swung.

At the last second, Theo grasped his staff with two hands to block the attack, but his positioning was off. The full weight of the mace crashed into his staff, and the wood snapped with a splintering crack.

Theo immediately cast it aside and sprinted toward the closest chest. A few paces from it, he dropped to his knees, sliding through the dirt to reach it faster, even if only by a second. He thrust open the lid, revealing a variety of battle axes. He grabbed one right as Lahmi's fingers locked into his hair and yanked him back. Theo twisted and swung, clipping the giant's arm with his blade.

Lahmi howled in pain, reached down with a massive hand, and grasped Theo by the collar of his shirt, then threw him across the stadium as if he were a doll.

His body slammed into the arena wall. Spectators leaned over, some cheering, some jeering. Those in the front row slammed their open palms against the barrier. The vibration of their pounding pulsed in Theo's body, syncing with the thrumming energy that coursed through his veins.

Theo's head swam. He sat up, dizzy, seeing Lahmi five yards to his left with Theo's battle axe at his feet. Ten yards to his right, he saw the only other unopened battle chest.

"Wolf!" He heard a voice shout above the crowd.

Theo jerked his head up to see William and his men. Annelee stood beside them, knuckles white as she clenched her hands together in front of her.

Theo's gaze drifted back to Lahmi, who was now holding both the mace and the battle axe. He swung each one in a circle, one-handed.

"Get up, Wolf! Get up!"

William's voice rang in Theo's pounding head. He staggered to his feet.

Lahmi sauntered toward him, flashing a blood-thirsty grin. As he approached, Theo could see that his teeth had been filed into fangs.

"Move!" This time it was Annelee who shouted. "Move, Theo!"

The sound of her voice screaming his name awakened something inside him. Once again, Theo focused on the explosion of energy in his body. This time, it raged like an inferno, like a fire shut up in his bones. He couldn't hold it in.

He sprinted toward the final chest and threw open the lid. His eyes landed on the sword that sat atop the pile of weapons. Five gemstones glittered on the hilt: a diamond, an emerald, an onyx, a ruby, and another diamond.

"White," Theo whispered. "Green, black, red, and white."

The words unlocked a deeper strength he didn't know he had.

He wrapped his fingers around the hilt. The cold metal sent a jolt up his arm.

Hearing Lahmi's footsteps, he turned and swung.

The giant blocked the blow, awakening another burst of images in Theo's mind. But this time, Theo used them. The pictures flashed so fast, he could hardly make sense of them.

A dusty library …

Desert sands …

Black-winged beasts …

Theo's feet moved instinctively, propelling his body toward the giant with ever-increasing speed. His arms swung, arcing and stabbing his sword as if it were the only thing he'd ever learned to do.

As if he'd been born for war.

He swung again.

A piercing shriek echoed through the stadium.

Lahmi clutched a bloody stump where his hand had been. Both battle axe and mace lay abandoned on the ground.

Without another thought, Theo charged the giant. He jumped into the air and spun, executing a perfect spinning back kick. His foot landed in the giant's chest, but Theo's body didn't stop. The momentum knocked Lahmi to the ground.

The roar of the crowd rose to a deafening level as Theo stomped a booted foot into the giant's gut and thrust the tip of his sword at his neck. He stopped the blade an inch shy of the kill and stared into the beastly man's eyes.

Blue eyes.

An image of a boy flashed through Theo's mind. A sound like a laugh echoed in his memory.

The giant blinked. "Finish me," he growled.

Theo's fingers tightened around the hilt of the sword. He pulled back slightly, as if about to thrust all of his body weight against the blade and into Lahmi's neck.

But those eyes.

So familiar.

He couldn't shake it.

In one swift motion, Theo withdrew his sword from Lahmi's neck and instead pierced the giant's fleshy thigh, pinning him to the ground.

Lahmi released an animalistic howl. He shrieked and reached for the sword with his good hand, trying to rip it from his thigh, but he couldn't reach the hilt.

Theo took a step back from his incapacitated rival. He held up both hands to quiet the crowd. When they'd fallen silent, he declared in a bold voice, "I will not kill this man!"

The crowd roared once again, and this time, Queen Naomi stood.

The audience quieted.

"Very well." Her rich voice carried through the stadium. "It's clear that though you chose to spare Lahmi's life, you could have taken it. Therefore, I hereby proclaim the outsider from Viren the winner of the Duellum Mortis!"

The crowd erupted.

Theo exhaled and dropped to his knees. All at once, the supernatural strength left his body, leaving behind a throbbing ache and a searing burn on his right shoulder.

He glanced over at the rebels, who cheered, "Wolf! Wolf! Wolf!"

Annelee stood, hands clutched at her chest, a look of relief evident on her striking face. Her gaze drifted toward the other side of the auditorium. She pointed a finger, and Theo turned.

In the box seat directly across from Naomi, Cain stood, huffed, then disappeared into the crowd.

An unsettling feeling washed over Theo, but he pushed it aside, instead focusing on the chant that now filled the stadium as every resident of Saxum cheered for his victory.

"Wolf! Wolf! Wolf!"

When he faced Annelee again, she'd joined in the cheer, thrusting a hand into the air. But as he read her lips, he could tell she sang a different chant.

"Theo! Theo! Theo!"

He returned her smile, placed his right hand over his heart, then thrust a fist into the sky, basking in his victory.

Theo was the victor.

Chapter Nine

THEO FOLLOWED the two guards who escorted him from the stadium back into Queen Naomi's throne room. Four sets of rebel arms immediately welcomed him with hugs and claps on the back.

"I knew you could do it!" Liam said, smacking Theo on the shoulder. "The Wolf!" He lifted Theo's hand and thrust it toward the sky. "The champion of Viren *and* Saxum!"

"Give the boy some space," William said. He greeted Theo with a firm handshake, clasping his hand around Theo's forearm. "Well done, Wolf. I'll admit, I wasn't as optimistic as Liam."

"Me either," Elijah said. "Did you see the size of that man?" He shook his head. "I definitely thought you were going to die."

"Yes, I certainly did see him," Theo said, glancing past William and the other rebels. Annelee stood at a distance, hands folded at her waist. "And he looked even bigger up close," Theo added.

"How'd you do it?" Conrad asked. "I've never seen anyone move the way you did."

Theo ignored the question, crossed the room, and approached Annelee. "Hi," he said.

She smiled. "Hi."

"So … I'm not dead." He chuckled.

Annelee nodded. "And for that I'm very grateful." She took a step closer and looked as if she was about to hug him. Instead, her eyes drifted past him, and she paused.

Theo turned to see the four rebel men staring and grinning.

A guard's voice interrupted the moment. "Please take a knee for Queen Naomi." He gestured to the door behind the throne. Naomi entered, then took her seat.

Her dark eyes found Theo's as she motioned for the rebels to rise. "Well done, young man. Never in all my years have I seen—"

"Sister!" Cain's voice bellowed through the doorway. His artificial good humor long gone, he stormed into the room, shot a glare at Theo, then faced Queen Naomi. Composing himself, he said, "I suppose congratulations are in order." He extended a hand to his sister.

She refused to shake it. Instead, she simply said,

"Thank you, Brother."

Cain withdrew his hand. "My men and I will be on our way soon. However, I thought it necessary to discuss the arrangements of our agreement post Duellum Mortis, seeing as both warriors still stand."

Naomi crossed her legs. "Both warriors are alive, but yours is far from standing. No, I will still send my army. My champion has clearly won."

Hope flickered in Theo's chest, then faded as he saw the flash of hatred on Cain's face.

"Fine," Cain said. He took a step closer to the throne. The guards in the room stiffened and placed their hands on their daggers. "Take your pitiful army down to Viren," he said in a low growl. "Let it be shredded and weakened. I'll be the vulture who picks your bones. Mark my words, Sister, you'll come back with your tail between your legs."

Cain scanned the rebel warriors with a final threatening stare, then stormed out of the throne room.

Naomi watched him leave, exhaled, then turned to William. "You and your team should get some rest. We'll leave at dawn for Viren."

William bowed. "Thank you, Your Highness."

"Don't thank me," she said. "Thank your champion." She flashed a rare smile at Theo, then stood to leave. "Guards, please escort them to the sleeping quarters."

William rounded up the rebels. "Look, I know we're all exhausted, but one of us must ride back to camp and send word to the rest of our people. This is a numbers game. We'll need every one of our warriors present if we are to intimidate Marsuuv into surrendering and releasing the prisoners."

"Say no more," Elijah said.

William nodded. "You'll need to leave now if you're to meet us outside the city in two-and-half days' time."

"I'll ride through the night," Elijah said with a nod.

"Thank you, my friend." William patted him on the back. "As for the rest of you," William said, searching the faces of his teammates. "It's time to rest."

Theo followed William and the other rebels out of the throne room and down the same long white hall they'd entered that morning. He slowed to match Annelee's pace, allowing more distance to form between them and the other rebels. Once they were several yards behind, Annelee touched his arm and motioned for him to lift his sleeve.

Theo cast a glance ahead and, once he was sure no one was watching, rolled it up.

Four empty black outlines marked his upper arm.

Only one of the five bars remained full.

He quickly pulled his sleeve back down to his wrist.

"I knew it," she whispered.

Theo glanced at her. In the minutes following the Duellum Mortis, he suspected that Annelee was correct about the curse, but he hadn't taken the time to confirm it until now. The more they used their special skills, the faster their bars faded.

"You have only one bar left," she whispered. "What are we going to do?"

He touched a hand to his shoulder. "You were right about them. I felt a supernatural strength out there. I could feel it coursing through my body."

She nodded. "I felt it too. When I shot that arrow. But how are we going to get to a Waystation in time for you?" She touched her shoulder. "And me."

"We'll be careful. You know, conserve our energy. Tomorrow, we'll ride to Viren and take our stand outside the city's walls. Marsuuv will surrender, and then we'll get to a Waystation."

Seeing the concern on her face and feeling brave after just having defeated a giant, Theo reached over and took Annelee's hand in his. He gave it a squeeze, interlocked his fingers with hers, and for the first time thought maybe this curse wasn't so bad after all.

Two-and-a-half days later, Theo and the other rebels

approached Viren, mere hours before the imprisoned people of their beloved kingdom were set to be executed. They'd already sent a messenger to the city to inform Marsuuv that Sir William Atwood sought audience with him and would meet him in the southern fields at first light.

They stopped just shy of the city near dawn. Theo sat atop his horse at the head of the army, directly behind William and Queen Naomi. Two hundred twenty bodies of sinew and strength—horses and warriors—poised in rows behind them, weapons sheathed but eyes and minds alert. The city walls loomed directly ahead beyond a grassy rise, no more than half a mile away.

Still no sign of Marsuuv.

An eerie calm settled over Theo as he took in the scene. Only the chirping of a few birds broke the silence.

"Look." Beside him, Annelee pointed.

The first sign of a Dark Rider appeared on the rise, followed by another.

"Here we go," she whispered.

Theo and Annelee locked eyes. "Everything's going to be okay. As soon as this is over, we ride to a Waystation."

Annelee glanced back at the ridge, where a dozen of Marsuuv's warriors gathered. "It can't be over soon enough." She touched the spot on her arm where the markings hid beneath her sleeve.

William turned and faced his newly expanded army. Nearly a dozen rows of warriors stretched behind them. Only nineteen were rebels, the rest were warriors from Saxum. Theo had to admit, the goat people were a sight to behold in their skins, war paint, and horned accessories.

William cleared his throat. "Look alive!"

Beside him, Conrad drew his sword.

"Not today, my friend," William said, motioning for Conrad to sheathe his weapon. Then louder, he said, "Remember, we shed no blood. Marsuuv's army is a mere fifty strong. We outnumber them four to one."

Queen Naomi turned and repeated the message in the native Saxum tongue.

Theo listened to the sound of her rich voice but fixed his eyes on the rise where all fifty Dark Riders now stood in formation.

"Uh, William …" Theo pointed.

From behind the fifty original Dark Riders appeared another fifty, maybe more.

"He must have converted more of the King's Guard," William said. "This changes nothing. We still outnumber them two to one. We ride." He gave a signal and the whole army moved forward as one unit, William and

Naomi in the lead.

The additional Dark Riders took up formation beside the others.

Then fifty more appeared.

William and Naomi pulled to a stop.

"What is this?" she demanded.

"I … I don't know," William stammered.

Yet another fifty Dark Riders emerged over the rise.

"Elyon help us," Naomi said under her breath.

Theo stared at her, once again feeling overcome by a strange sense of déjà vu. He didn't have time to ask her about this Elyon.

At least two hundred warriors darkened the hillside between them and the city walls.

"You said there were only fifty." She pointed. "But their numbers are nearly equal to ours."

"That's the entire King's Guard," Annelee said. "Marsuuv must've converted all of them."

"You assured me there would be no bloodshed," Naomi said, shooting daggers at William with her glare. "This is not what we agreed to."

William stared straight ahead but said nothing. His stunned silence unnerved Theo.

Behind them, whispers rippled through the Viren-Saxum army. The name *Cain* drifted from the back row to the front.

Theo maneuvered his horse and turned to see a rider approaching from behind them, an army in tow.

It was Cain.

The snap of horse's reins cracked through the air. Queen Naomi trotted past Theo toward the rear of their formation. The crowd of horses and warriors parted to allow her through. William followed.

"Let's go," Annelee said.

Theo followed, hearing Conrad behind him.

One hundred fifty of Cain's men took up formation behind the Viren-Saxum army. They were now caught between Marsuuv's Dark Riders and Cain's army. Cain sat erect atop his horse. Theo recognized Steffos beside him. Theo's heart caught in his throat.

Cain held up a hand to stay his warriors, then rode forward to meet Queen Naomi. Steffos and one other warrior joined him.

"Conrad, stay here with the army," William said. "You too, Hawk." He gestured to Annelee. "Don't be afraid to use your bow if something goes awry. Take Cain first with a long shot if you can. And remember, no Dark Riders if you can help it."

"Yes, sir." She touched the weapon on her shoulder and nodded. But when her eyes met Theo's, he knew she intended to do no such thing. Just as he had no intention of fighting. They had to conserve their strength, or their bars would vanish.

"Wolf, come with us." William motioned for Theo to follow, then rode with Naomi to meet Cain.

The queen spoke first. "Brother, what are you doing here?" Her voice held a hint of warning. "We had an agreement."

Theo swallowed, hoping Cain was about to say he'd had a change of heart and decided to back his sister in her stand against Marsuuv.

"We did have an agreement," Cain said. "But things have changed. I intended to let you come here and lose half your forces to Marsuuv and his Dark Riders." He smirked. "But a plan greater than mine was proposed, and I agreed."

"A plan made by whom?" Naomi demanded.

Cain's smirk spread into a full smile. "Why, Marsuuv, of course. One thing you'll learn, dear Sister: he's always five steps ahead." He fixed Theo with his stare. "You weren't supposed to survive the Duellum Mortis. Today you'll not be so lucky."

Theo swallowed.

"What's Marsuuv's obsession with the boy?" William demanded. "What could he possibly want with him?"

"It's not my concern *why* he wants the boy. Nor is it my concern *what* Marsuuv does with him once I deliver him."

"So this is why you chose him for the duel?" Naomi said. "To fulfill Marsuuv's wishes? Are you a puppet now, following his orders?"

Cain narrowed his eyes.

"Your actions speak though your lips do not." Naomi shook her head. "This is the kind of man you are now? A man who betrays his own flesh and blood at the whims of an outsider?"

"And this who you are now, Sister—a ruler who follows the plans of a lovestruck fool." Cain sneered at William. "Did you really believe you could march down here with a show of power and force Marsuuv to surrender?" He tsked. "It shows how little you know your enemy. Which is why he'll win."

William straightened in his saddle. "You would fight your own people to serve this monster?" he asked.

"He's not a monster," Cain said. "He's a god. And anyone too blind to see his true power is no longer fit to be called *my people*. But, Sister, as my flesh and blood, I'll give you one opportunity to retreat." He paused dramatically. "With your tail between your legs. Just as I prophesied." He laughed. "Retreat. Flee with your army back to Saxum and live to fight another day with me." He stared at William and growled. "Today, my battle is against the rebels not with you."

Theo's stomach dropped. He touched his arm,

knowing he had less than one full bar left, Annelee two.

Cain interrupted his thoughts. "Well, Sister, I'll give you a moment to decide the fate of your people. After that …" He raised his eyebrows. "We'll slaughter all who remain. Choose wisely."

Cain locked eyes with Theo, then spit.

Theo turned to see Annelee, Conrad, and their now outnumbered army. From the look on her face, Theo knew she was thinking the same thing as him.

They were never going to make it to a Waystation.

Chapter Ten

THEO FOLLOWED William and Queen Naomi as they rode back to meet their army. HeHe pulled his horse to a stop alongside Annelee's.

"What happened?" she whispered.

Before he could answer, Conrad asked the same question of William. "What happened over there? What did Cain have to say? Did he decide to align with us after all?"

"No," Theo answered. "He's here to fight for Marsuuv."

Annelee's eyes widened.

Naomi muttered something under her breath.

"Don't let your brother scare you," William said to her.

She scoffed. "Of course I'm scared—for the people who stand with me *and* with him. You should be too. You don't know what he's capable of." She stared at the Viren-Saxum army. "You, Sir William Atwood, came into my throne room and said you wouldn't fight against your own people. What kind of queen would I be if I were willing to do the very thing you are not?"

"Surely there's another option," Conrad said.

"There is," Naomi responded. "And I'm taking it."

"Don't," William said.

"What?" Conrad demanded.

Naomi glanced between the two men. "I must. I'm taking my army and returning to Saxum."

"You can't!" William objected. "We'll be slaughtered!"

Empathy washed over her face as she sucked in a deep breath. "I have no other choice. I'm sorry you find yourself in this predicament." She leaned back, brought her fingers to her lips, and let out a rapid staccato of piercing whistles to signal to her lieutenants. They returned the whistle, then shouted, "Retreat!"

Naomi pulled her horse alongside William's, leaned over, and touched his arm. In a low voice, she said, "Don't be foolish." Theo saw the intensity in her eyes. "Run!" She snapped her horse's reins, then headed north. Row by row, the entire Saxum army followed her. Only William's rebels lingered, confusion in their eyes.

William watched the retreating army as if in a trance, his face pale.

"What do we do now?" Conrad asked. He looked to the western horizon in the direction of their camp.

"Even if we run, how can we expect to make it out of here? We're surrounded."

Theo stared in the same direction as William, watching as their army dwindled from two hundred to twenty, his stomach sinking deeper with each Saxum warrior who vanished over the horizon. Heat flared across his shoulder. Instinctively, Theo touched it, feeling warmth beneath his sleeve. He turned to face Annelee.

She mouthed, *What are we going to do?*

Theo shook his head. Time seemed to slow as he considered their options. Everything inside him screamed at him to run, to flee to the nearest Waystation with Annelee and save themselves. But even if that didn't draw an immediate target on their backs, he wouldn't abandon the Kingdom of Viren—especially not when the Dark Riders who'd murdered his parents were somewhere among the crowd.

The remnant of rebels rode to meet them. As if on cue, the Dark Riders began their advance from the east. Cain's Defectors closed in from the west, unhurried. There was no doubt about how this would go.

Conrad repeated the same question. "William, what do we do now? We're waiting for your orders."

William stared unblinkingly at the advancing armies.

"William?" Conrad said louder. "William!"

The future prince of Viren mumbled, "I uh … we should …"

Theo's mind whirled, trying to formulate a plan that would allow him and Annelee to get to a Waystation without abandoning their entire army. He pressed his hand against the marks on his arm, feeling their warmth through his sleeve. He closed his eyes, feeling his own draining life force urge him to run south. His eyes flew open. He knew where to find the next Waystation. And if there was any hope of making it, they'd have to flee now.

"William!" Conrad snapped his fingers in his commander's face.

"Retreat," Theo said to Conrad. "South to the forest. If we can make it there, we might stand a chance of escape through the trees. We're sitting ducks in this open field."

Conrad glanced between William and Theo.

"*You* have to make the call," Theo said.

Conrad gave a swift nod, then shouted, "Retreat! Retreat to the south! To the forest!" He snapped his reins and took off at a gallop.

William shook his head, locked eyes with Theo, then shouted, "Retreat!"

The sound of horses' hooves pounded behind Theo as he took off after William and Conrad. Annelee raced at his side, her short black hair whipping her face as the tiny rebel army drove their horses south.

Theo fixed his eyes straight ahead at the thickest growth of the southern forest. In the trees, they might stand a chance—he and the other rebels had been navigating the woods for weeks. They weren't as familiar with the southern terrain, but surely they'd be harder to pick off while darting through trees than sitting out in an open field.

Theo focused on the rhythm of his horse's hooves, the pant of its breath. He urged her forward, pushing her harder. He leaned over her neck to streamline his body.

A surge of black to his left caught his attention. From the eastern ridge outside the city, nearly a hundred of the Dark Riders rushed south.

"Dark Riders!" he shouted to Conrad and William. "To the east! They're going to cut us off at the forest!"

"Not if we get there first!" William called back.

A quick glance over Theo's shoulder revealed the rest of the Dark Riders closing in, encircling them from the east. Cain and his warriors did the same, racing in formation to block their escape to the west and north.

Theo reached for the hilt of his sword. Despite William's every effort, they'd never make it without a fight. Ahead of him, he saw the future prince of Viren draw his weapon. Even Annelee gripped her bow. Theo unsheathed his sword and caught her gaze.

The Dark Riders moved at an unnatural speed, swiftly closing formation. In seconds, the rebels' path of escape would be blocked.

A glance over Theo's right shoulder revealed Cain's Defectors closing. He straightened in his saddle and lifted his sword, feeling a swell of familiar energy course through his body.

The same energy that had secured his victory in the Duellum Mortis.

Realizing they were out of options, Theo pressed into the power, preparing to unleash every skill in his warrior arsenal.

Seeing Annelee nock an arrow, he shouted to her. "Let's hope you're right about these things!" He gripped his sword in his right hand and tapped his marked shoulder with his left. "Because we're going to need every ounce of strength we can get!"

Chapter Eleven

THE FIRST DARK RIDERS broke away from the pack, cutting off Conrad, then William. The sound of metal against metal rang through the air.

Seconds later, two of Marsuuv's warriors cut hard across the field and drove their horses straight at Theo, swords drawn. He sucked in a sharp breath, shot one last look at Annelee, then pushed his horse forward, barely dodging their blades.

Ahead of him, a wall of riders blocked the path to the forest. Steadying his breath, he focused his thoughts on the swell of unnatural power that coursed through his veins, the same strength he'd used to defeat the giant Lahmi.

Another rider broke formation, drawing Theo's attention to the right. He almost didn't see the armor-clad man who came at him from the left.

Arcing his sword, he steadied himself as his blade

clanged against another. The blow reverberated up his arm, but he swung again, this time clipping a Dark Rider's shoulder. Following the impulses of his body, Theo swung right without even looking. His blade rang out as he blocked another attack.

Ahead, the line of Dark Riders dispersed to isolate each rebel. Theo rushed for the tree line, but when he was nearly there, an overwhelming sense of dread washed over him. He pulled his horse around, denying every instinct that shouted at him to keep going. Instead, he turned back. His eyes landed on the distinct outline of Marsuuv standing on the nearby ridge, watching.

"Why isn't he fighting?" Theo wondered aloud, but the sound of Annelee's battle cry pulled his attention back toward the trees. He couldn't see her through the blur of horses and humans.

Before rejoining the fight, he cast one final look at Marsuuv.

The man had vanished.

A familiar stench caught Theo's nose. The overpowering smell of goat musk filled the air. He urged his horse forward, but the smell grew stronger.

Feeling a swell of power in his arms, Theo pressed his palms against the saddle to lift his body, then swung his legs over the horse's rump and spun around in one swift movement. Now facing backward, he saw Cain's army closing in behind him, Steffos in the lead. The man flashed his teeth at Theo, sword drawn and closing fast.

Theo's body came alive as the warrior's mount caught his own.

He swung.

Steffos blocked his strike, but Theo knew he would. He leaped up onto his saddle, balancing on the balls of his feet in a crouched position. As Steffos moved to strike again, Theo launched himself from the back of his horse, directly at the man.

Steffos let out a grunt as Theo crashed into him, knocking the man from his saddle and disarming him at the same time. Now armed with two swords, Theo sprinted for his mare who had pulled up, leaped onto its back, and took off again toward the forest, throwing one of the blades to knock an archer's bow from his hands. Liam, who'd been the target, nodded to Theo as he rode past.

Ahead of him, Annelee stood on the back of her horse, masterfully balancing while the beast galloped. She nocked an arrow and took aim, hitting a Dark Rider in the shoulder. Dropping back down to her seat, her horse broke the tree line. Theo raced into the forest behind her.

Searing heat flared across his shoulder as he dodged trees. Thinking he'd been struck, Theo turned, but no one was there. He gasped in pain again. For a second, he felt disoriented. He pushed up his sleeve to reveal all but a sliver of his last bar now gone.

An arrow whipped past his head with mere inches to spare. His eyes found the source: a Dark Rider ten yards ahead and closing, his next arrow already aimed.

Theo yanked his sleeve back down and locked eyes with the man, but before he could loose his arrow, Annelee rushed into view on horseback, riding in from the left. A few feet before colliding with the Dark Rider, she pulled her horse up short, leaped from its back, and grasped a tree branch overhead. She swung her booted feet into the man's chest, knocking him to the earth.

Another one of Cain's warriors pulled up behind her with blade drawn just as she dropped to the ground. Theo threw his sword past Annelee's head and knocked the man's weapon from his hand. Before the enemy could make another move, Theo rushed toward Annelee, offering her a hand as his horse galloped past. He pulled her up into the saddle behind him.

"Thanks!" she panted.

"Still got some arrows?"

"Plenty."

"Good," he said, ripping his hunting knife from the

sheath at his waist. "Fire away."

The sound of the snapping bowstring resonated in Theo's ears. Through the trees ahead, he saw Annelee's riderless horse. He pushed his mare to catch up to it.

"Here," he said, handing her the reins. "I'm going to take your horse and double back to get my sword." Before she could respond, he leaped from one horse to the other and threw the knife. The blade met its mark in a Defector's chest. "Stay alive!" he shouted. And not caring who heard, he added, "And get to a Waystation!"

Theo found his sword no more than twenty yards back. But by the time he snatched it up and looked around, the battle had dispersed. There was no sign of his rebel comrades, nor the Dark Riders and Defectors. Only a disturbing silence and sinister calm. A chill snaked down his back. He ignored it and took off in the direction where he'd left Annelee. She wouldn't be that far ahead of him. Gripping tight to the reins of her horse, Theo turned his focus inward, searching for the instinct that would lead him to the Waystation. The skin of his right shoulder burned.

He touched a finger to his shoulder. An image of a white-domed building flashed through his mind.

"This way," he said to Annelee's horse, pushing her southward.

Wind rustled the leaves overhead. Clouds rolled

in and masked the sun in gloom. A gust of cold air exhaled through the trees and whipped Theo's hair.

Another unsettling wave of dread washed over him.

He pushed the horse harder.

An animal's scream shattered the eerie calm. Theo recognized the sound.

Coming around a thicket of trees, he saw his own horse rearing on its hind legs.

Annelee was not on its back.

The horse's front hooves crashed back down to the earth with a thud, then it took off at a gallop.

A second later, another scream rang out through the forest. Again, Theo recognized it. But this time it wasn't an animal.

It was Annelee.

A wave of nausea rolled through Theo's body.

"Annelee!" he shouted, then galloped off in the direction of the sound.

Pain slashed his right shoulder. His stomach churned with sickness. But now Theo knew it wasn't from the fear of what might happen to Annelee.

His life force was fading.

Faintness was overtaking his head, but Theo ignored it.

He had to get to Annelee before his curse was sealed.

Theo's heart thrummed. His lungs burned. Vision blurred in and out of focus as he crashed through the trees, following an even deeper instinct than the draw of the Waystation. Annelee's presence pulled him toward her.

Sweat beaded his brow as he fought the desire to close his eyes and give in to the pain.

"Come on, girl," he said to the horse and dug his heels into her sides.

Another shriek sliced through the forest. Theo knew he was close. Pushing the horse one final time, he broke through the trees into a small clearing. He immediately jerked the mare to a stop.

A pale-faced, black-clad man stood at the far edge, dagger in one hand, Annelee's arm gripped in the other.

"Marsuuv," Theo breathed.

"Run!" Annelee shouted. "Save yourself!"

"Silence!" The man hissed. He shook his head, and the black hood fell back from his face, revealing the white skin of his bald head. A network of thin black veins spiderwebbed across his scalp.

"Theo! Get out of here!"

"Let her go!" Theo demanded, while clutching his aching chest.

Marsuuv pressed the dagger to Annelee's throat. "I don't think so." Releasing her arm with his other hand, Marsuuv gripped the fabric of Annelee's shirt and ripped the sleeve.

Four black outlines marked her shoulder beneath one remaining full bar.

Marsuuv trailed the thin fingers of his free hand over the markings. "I know who you are," he said in a low voice, eyes fixed on Theo as he spoke.

The phrase stirred something in Theo's mind. His words sounded familiar.

"I know who you are too," Theo said, struggling to get the words out. He couldn't shake the feeling that he'd said the phrase once before, that he'd seen this man's face before.

If he even was a man.

Theo's mind drifted back to their days in the Kingdom of Saxum. Something Cain had said returned to him.

"He's not just one man," Theo whispered under his breath. His thoughts swirled. "He's not just one man!" Theo shouted, delirious. He swayed in the saddle. "He's not just one …"

He gasped, unable to finish.

Marsuuv chuckled. "No matter what costume you wear, I will know you." The sound of his voice carved daggers of fire into Theo's shoulder, but the words didn't make sense. Pain spread through his arm like poison, then blossomed in his chest.

An icy cold replaced the fiery pain as the final drops of Theo's life force drained from his body.

He saw Marsuuv's lips move, but this time, he couldn't hear the voice over the sound of his own fading heartbeat thrumming in his ears.

Sucking in a ragged breath, Theo managed to breathlessly say, "I'm … sorry … I'm sorry, Annelee."

"Theo! No! Stay with me, Theo!" Her voice sounded garbled, as if she were underwater.

As if he were underwater.

Theo tried to suck in air, but his lungs collapsed.

Faintness overtook him.

A sneer formed on Marsuuv's thin lips as he pressed the knife harder against Annelee's neck. She winced in pain.

It was the last thing Theo saw as darkness closed in on his periphery.

His body lurched in the saddle, then spasmed.

Succumbing to the faintness, Theo collapsed forward onto the horse and drowned in Marsuuv's curse.

Chapter Twelve

NOOO!" ANNELEE SCREAMED. The sound of her own voice terrified her as she watched Theo collapse against the neck of his horse. "Theo! Wake up! Wake up!"

Marsuuv released her arm from his cold, bony fingers and lowered the dagger from her neck. He sheathed the weapon, then ripped her satchel from her shoulder and began digging through the contents.

Annelee seized the opportunity and ran toward Theo's horse.

In a flash of black and inhuman speed, Marsuuv blocked her path. Ice filled Annelee's veins as she stared into the haunting eyes of the man who'd cursed her. She couldn't shake the feeling that she'd stared into those eyes once before.

"Ah, ah, ah," Marsuuv said in a lyrical voice. "I don't remember dismissing you."

In one swift motion, he grasped Annelee by the collar with his talonlike hands, then tossed her across the clearing. Her back slammed against the trunk of a tree. With a loud groan, she collapsed to the ground and rolled over onto her side, watching as Marsuuv continued his search through her satchel.

He yanked out a wrapped parcel of jerky and dropped it onto the ground, followed by an apple and a small canteen that landed with a loud slosh. When he found the quill she used to write in her journal, he paused, twirling it between his fingers.

Annelee's gaze drifted to Theo. He hadn't moved, and from what she could tell, he wasn't breathing. She scanned the surroundings, her mind whirling to come up with a plan.

A soft chuckle redirected her attention to Marsuuv, who stood in the center of the clearing, holding her leather-bound journal. A sinister smirk flickered across his thin lips, then disappeared.

"This one is powerless," he said, then tossed the journal in Annelee's direction. It landed with a thump; its pages splayed open. Her eyes scanned the text.

White, green, black, red, and white.

Her eyes trailed the words, still not understanding what they meant, even though she'd read them countless times during their recent travels.

Chapter Twelve

Beneath the list of colors, in her own handwriting, were the words *Remember. Remember who you are.*

Below that: *Human blood is poison to Shataiki.*

And finally: *What if our skills are connected to our life force?*

A sound drew her attention back to Marsuuv, who approached Theo.

She spotted her bow and quiver leaning against a tree. She'd never reach it, not before Marsuuv noticed, and certainly not when he could move with inhuman speed.

He's not just one man.

Theo's words echoed in her mind.

"He's not just one man," Annelee whispered to herself.

She watched him lift Theo's sleeve and examine the five black outlines on his right shoulder.

"And what if he's not a man at all?" she said in a faint voice.

She shot a quick glance at her bare arm where Marsuuv had torn her sleeve. She had one bar left. It would have to be enough. And if her theory was correct, she was at the height of her skills.

Across the clearing, Theo's horse tried to back away from Marsuuv. He grabbed the reins to steady it and reached into the saddlebag.

Annelee gave the area a final scan, her warrior's mind calculating her next move. Drawing her knees to her chest, she curled her body silently, rolled into a crouching position, then sprang into action. Using every ounce of strength in her legs, Annelee sprang vertically, flung her arms up, grabbed the branch over her head, and swung up into the tree.

As soon as her feet touched the bouncing limb, she sprang again, this time leaping through the air toward the nearest tree. She caught a limb with plenty of momentum to flip over it and vault her body several yards through the air towards her bow. When she landed, it was at her feet, and Marsuuv was staring at her.

In the span of a breath, Annelee snatched an arrow from its quiver, and dragged its sharp head across her palm. Crimson red liquid pooled in her hand and coated the blade.

Red, she heard in her mind as she nocked the arrow. *Sacrifice.*

Not knowing what it meant, she took aim, then loosed the blood-tipped projectile.

It streaked across the clearing and sank into Marsuuv's torso.

He gasped, wavered on his feet for a second, then dropped to his knees, wide eyes on the arrow. Black smoke curled from the wound in his gut.

Annelee sprinted toward Theo with a speed she didn't know she had, leaped onto the back of the horse behind him, then snapped the reins. The mare took off at a full gallop.

She cast a final glance over her shoulder to see Marsuuv hunched over his wound. He reached around to his back and yanked the arrow out the other side. A smile formed on his lips but was quickly hidden behind the thin trail of black smoke that seeped from the hole in his gut.

Horrified, Annelee looked away and wrapped her arms around Theo to keep him from falling.

"I've got you," she said as she urged the horse into a run.

She gripped his body tighter, trying to ignore the sinister chuckle that reached out for her through the trees.

"I'll get us to a Waystation," she breathed.

She hoped she was right.

*To be continued in the next book
of the Dream Traveler's Game:*

BOOK SEVEN
OUT OF THE DARKNESS

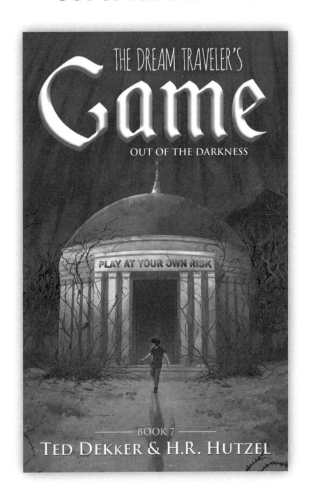

MORE ADVENTURES AWAIT

Discover the entire
Dekker young reader universe.

WWW.TEDDEKKER.COM

WWW.TEDDEKKER.COM